RAFE

RAFE

TEXAS BOUDREAU BROTHERHOOD

By

KATHY IVAN

COPYRIGHT

Rafe – Original Copyright © March 2020 by Kathy Ivan

Cover by Elizabeth Mackay of EMGRAPHICS

Release date: March 2020
Print Edition

All Rights Reserved

RAFE – Texas Boudreau Brotherhood

When Sheriff Rafe Boudreau catches Tessa Maxwell climbing through the window of a house where she doesn't belong, the crime rate isn't the only thing that spikes. Turns out, trouble has followed the small-town schoolteacher to Shiloh Springs, and Rafe and the rest of the Boudreau clan must step in to keep her safe. Can they decipher the clues and end the danger Tessa faces before time runs out?

BOOKS BY KATHY IVAN

www.kathyivan.com/books.html

TEXAS BOUDREAU BROTHERHOOD
Rafe

Antonio

Brody

Lucas

Heath (coming soon)

NEW ORLEANS CONNECTION SERIES
Desperate Choices

Connor's Gamble

Relentless Pursuit

Ultimate Betrayal

Keeping Secrets

Sex, Lies and Apple Pies

Deadly Justice

Wicked Obsession

Hidden Agenda

Spies Like Us

Fatal Intentions

New Orleans Connection Series Box Set: Books 1-3

New Orleans Connection Series Box Set: Books 4-7

CAJUN CONNECTION SERIES
Saving Sarah

Saving Savannah

Saving Stephanie

Guarding Gabi

LOVIN' LAS VEGAS SERIES
It Happened In Vegas

Crazy Vegas Love

Marriage, Vegas Style

A Virgin In Vegas

Vegas, Baby!

Yours For The Holidays

Match Made In Vegas

One Night In Vegas

Last Chance In Vegas

Lovin' Las Vegas (box set books 1-3)

OTHER BOOKS BY KATHY IVAN
Second Chances (Destiny's Desire Book #1)

Losing Cassie (Destiny's Desire Book #2)

Dear Reader,

Welcome to Shiloh Springs, Texas! Don't you just love a small Texas town, where the people are neighborly, the gossip plentiful, and the heroes are …well, heroic, not to mention easy on the eyes! I love everything about Texas, which I why I've made the great state my home for over thirty years. There's no other place like it. From the delicious Tex-Mex food and downhome barbecue, the majestic scenery, and downhome atmosphere, the people and places of the Lone Star state are as unique and colorful as you'll find anywhere.

The Texas Boudreau Brotherhood series centers around a group of foster brothers, men who would have ended up in the system if not for Douglas and Patricia Boudreau. Instead of being hardened by life and circumstances beyond their control, they found a family who loved and accepted them, and gave them a place to call home. Sometimes brotherhood is more than sharing the same DNA.

If you've read my other romantic suspense books (the New Orleans Connection series and Cajun Connection series), you'll be familiar with the Boudreau name. Turns out there are a whole lot of Boudreaus out there, just itching to have their stories told. (Douglas is the brother of Gator Boudreau, patriarch of the New Orleans branch of the Boudreau family.)

So, sit back and relax. The pace of small-living might be less hectic than the big city, but small towns hold secrets, excitement, and heroes to ride to the rescue. And who doesn't love a Texas cowboy?

Kathy Ivan

EDITORIAL REVIEWS

"Kathy Ivan's books are addictive, you can't read just one."

—Susan Stoker, NYT Bestselling Author

"Kathy Ivan's books give you everything you're looking for and so much more."

—Geri Foster, USA Today and NYT Bestselling Author of the Falcon Securities Series

"In Shiloh Springs, Kathy Ivan has crafted warm, engaging characters that will steal your heart and a mystery that will keep you reading to the very last page."

—Barb Han, *USA TODAY* and Publisher's Weekly Bestselling Author

"This is the first I have read from Kathy Ivan and it won't be the last."

—Night Owl Reviews

"I highly recommend Desperate Choices. Readers can't go wrong here!"

—Melissa, Joyfully Reviewed

"I loved how the author wove a very intricate storyline with plenty of intriguing details that led to the final reveal…"

—Night Owl Reviews

Desperate Choices—Winner 2012 International Digital Award—Suspense

Desperate Choices—Best of Romance 2011 –Joyfully Reviewed

DEDICATIONS AND ACKNOWLEDGEMENTS

To my sister, Mary Sullivan, for her unwavering belief that I can write good stories. She keeps me focused, prodding me when I need it, and bopping me upside the head when I'm being lazy. This book is also dedicated to my mother, Betty Sullivan. She instilled in me the joy of reading at an early age and a love of romance, no matter the genre. I'd also like to thank Chris Keniston and Barb Han, who helped with writing blurbs, encouraging me, and helping keep my on track when I'd wander off in my own little world, chasing rabbits down rabbit holes.

More about Kathy and her books can be found at

WEBSITE:
www.kathyivan.com

Follow Kathy on Facebook at
www.facebook.com/kathyivanauthor

Follow Kathy on Twitter at
twitter.com/@kathyivan

Follow Kathy at BookBub
bookbub.com/profile/kathy-ivan

NEWSLETTER SIGN UP

Don't want to miss out on any new books, contests, and free stuff? Sign up to get my newsletter. I promise not to spam you, and only send out notifications/e-mails whenever there's a new release or contest/giveaway. Follow the link and join today!

http://eepurl.com/baqdRX

RAFE

By
KATHY IVAN

CHAPTER ONE

Pausing at the edge of the worn sidewalk, Tessa Maxwell contemplated the house she'd agreed to rent, sight unseen. Well, not exactly unseen. She'd viewed photos the realtor e-mailed her, but they didn't quite match the overgrown bushes and chipped paint on the shutters. But it would be okay—*it had to be.* Driving cross-country from Charlotte, North Carolina, she'd spent the last three days hauling a rented trailer behind her car, which contained almost everything she owned in the world. The few things she'd left behind at her sister's place would be shipped once she settled into her new life in Texas.

When she'd first pulled in front of the cottage, she spotted the honeysuckle wildly climbing along the side of the porch, overflowing a plastic garden trellis somebody had nailed on the side of the wide front porch. Up close, the fragrance from the white and yellow flowers evoked a sense of nostalgia, along with a touch of melancholy. Her mother had always worn a perfume with undertones of honeysuckle. She brushed at her eyes to keep the tears from overflowing.

No. No sad thoughts today.

Climbing the two steps leading to the porch, she ran her hand across the top of the wooden railing. Missing a couple of spindles, it resembled a kid who'd lost their two front teeth. At least a couple treads felt loose and threatened to collapse beneath her feet. Nothing she couldn't remedy with a hammer, a few nails, and a bit of elbow grease.

The overgrown shrubbery was lush and thick, and definitely in need of a good scalping, but the slightly bedraggled appearance of the old place didn't faze her. As long as the roof didn't leak, and the four walls remained intact, she'd make do.

Glancing at her watch, her lips twisted in a grimace. The realtor's e-mail stated she'd meet her at five, and it was already a quarter after with no sign of anybody around. *Which might be a bit of a problem. That last drive-through extra-large salted caramel Frappuccino had definitely tipped the scale over into one frap too many.*

Walking across the front porch, she grabbed the doorknob and twisted, praying it was unlocked. If luck was with her, she could sneak inside and take care of business before the realtor showed up. Heck, this was the middle of Podunk, Texas—didn't everybody leave their front doors unlocked here? The last thing she wanted was to get caught doing the potty dance in front of a total stranger her very first day in town. She chuckled as the image of her squatting behind the bushes sprang to life. The newspaper headline seemed obvious—new schoolteacher caught with her pants down—

literally.

When the knob didn't turn beneath her hand, she nibbled her lower lip. *Maybe I should text the realtor, and find out what's keeping her? Or tell her I have to leave, and I'll be back? Because I'm not sure how much longer I can hold it.*

Her gaze landed on the window by the front door. Old fashioned, like the cottage itself, it was one of those that slid up from the bottom. Perfect. She grinned, grabbed onto the edge of the white-painted wood, and gave a sharp upward tug. It moved slightly beneath her fingertips, and she wiggled her tush in a happy dance.

Maybe all wasn't lost.

With another hard tug and a bit of wrestling, she got the window halfway open, mentally crossing her fingers it was wide enough to squeeze through. Just her luck, she couldn't seem to get the stupid thing to open any farther. Plus, every time she let go of the pane, it slid a little downward.

Stupid window.

Grabbing onto the ledge, she wriggled and shimmied, managing to get her head and upper shoulders through the narrow opening. So far, so good.

Oh, well, here goes nothing.

Easing from the front seat of his pickup, Sheriff Rafe Boudreau left the truck's door ajar, not wanting to spook the intruder currently trespassing and jimmying open the window of the old Johnson house. Overgrown shrubbery obscured the lower half of his would-be felon, but the view of the upper half had the corners of his mouth tugging upward.

Long auburn hair hung down the center of her back, partially escaping from one of those elastic poufy things she'd used to tie it back. And his little cat burglar was definitely a female. A light blue T-shirt fit snugly, encasing a deliciously curvy figure. He couldn't help noticing her struggles with the old wood-framed window, which stubbornly refused to stay open, no matter how high up she pushed it. Not surprising in a house as old as the Johnson place, especially since it had sat vacant for most of the last year.

A softly muttered curse floated from the porch, and he bit back a chuckle. *Looks like my trespasser is struggling with the* entering *part of the whole breaking and entering thing.*

"Here I thought my jail cell would be sitting empty tonight. Guess I need to rethink that."

At his words, the intruder jumped, banging her head against the windowsill with an audible thump. Straightening, she rubbed at the spot, and glared at him with the prettiest blue eyes he'd ever seen. Surrounded by dark lashes, they reminded him of the sapphires in the ring his dad gave to Ms. Patti on their last anniversary.

Lush, full lips compressed into a line of pain. Despite that, his little thief was definitely easy on the eyes.

"I'm not breaking in. I live here—or I will as soon as the

realtor shows up with the keys."

Pretty, smart, and obviously thinks fast on her feet. Maybe she's done this kind of thing before, but she won't get away with it here—not in my town.

"House isn't for sale, or old Darrell Johnson would've mentioned it. Which means, I get to haul you in for trespassing, plus breaking and entering."

Crossing her arms, she gave him a thorough once over, and he stood silent, letting her look her fill. He'd been headed home after working a double shift, and had changed clothes at the station. He wasn't in uniform, instead wearing a faded pair of jeans, a plaid cotton shirt, and his favorite pair of cowboy boots. A dark Stetson shaded his eyes, but he still managed to see her, perfectly outlined against the porch's faded paint. He'd spent the better part of the day dealing with trivial misdemeanors and the ever-expanding pile of paperwork on his desk, and had been on his way home, planning on a quiet evening with a cold beer and maybe finding an action flick on the TV, when he'd spotted movement outside a house he knew stood empty.

Would she continue to bluff her way out of being hauled to the sheriff's office, or try to talk her way outta being charged? He'd play along—for now.

"I don't know who you think you are, Mister, and frankly I don't give a rat's patootie. I rented this place a week ago, and I am supposed to meet with," she paused before reaching into the front pocket of her jeans, and pulled out a piece of paper, "Serena Snowden, at five o'clock, to receive the keys."

Well, didn't that beat all? Either she was a very well-prepared thief, or she was telling the truth. He hadn't heard Old Man Johnson had finally agreed to rent out the empty house.

Reaching into his pocket, he pulled out his cell phone. Might as well give Serena a call and verify Red's alibi. Plus, he admitted, his curiosity was piqued by the feisty woman standing in front of him. The sound of car tires crunching against gravel drew his gaze to the drive, and he spotted Serena's white sedan pulling onto the driveway. A petite brunette stepped from the car and leaned back in, grabbing a briefcase.

Looks like Red's telling the truth.

He bit back a chuckle when he realized what it meant. Since he lived only a few houses further down the street, it looked like she was his new neighbor. "Afternoon, Serena."

"Rafe. What're you doing here?" Her worried gaze shifted between him and his pretty thief. Pushing back his hat, he couldn't stop grinning. Red glowered at him, and he had the feeling she'd like nothing better than to take a chunk outta his hide. More intrigued now than before, he wondered what brought her to town, and exactly who she was.

"Caught this little lady red-handed, crawling through Old Man Johnson's front window."

Serena's brow rose and she glanced at the other woman. "Ms. Maxwell?" He watched Red nod. "Sorry I'm late. I got caught up with a problem at the office. I know I should have called, but I was hoping I'd get here before you arrived."

"No problem. I couldn't wait to see inside the place." Though her words were pleasant enough, with his job and training, Rafe instinctively knew there was something more beneath her banal statement. She'd seemed a little too anxious to get into the house. Enough she'd risked climbing through a window. What the heck was up with that?

"I've got the keys right here." Serena held up a keyring with two shiny silver keys attached. "Why don't we head inside and do a quick walk through?"

"Sounds great." Red—no, wait, Serena had called her Ms. Maxwell—shifted from left to right, her body practically vibrating, anxious to get inside.

"Rafe, I've got this if you want to get home. I appreciate you checking things out, though." Serena smiled at him, and he knew he'd been dismissed. She'd shifted from family friend into businesswoman mode, the consummate professional ready to seal the deal, and he got the distinct impression he'd be in the way. A shame, because he really wanted to find out a bit more about the intriguing Ms. Maxwell.

It wouldn't take much to know everything he needed to about his new neighbor. He'd simply ask his mother. If there was one person in Shiloh Springs with their finger on the pulse of everything happening in their town, sometimes even before it happened, it was Patti Boudreau. He'd have answers by morning on Shiloh Springs's newest resident.

"No problem, sugar. Just doing my job. You ladies have a nice evening." Touching the brim of his Stetson, he turned and jogged down the steps and back to his truck.

Looked like things might be looking up in Shiloh Springs, and he couldn't wait.

CHAPTER TWO

Walking back into the main living room, Tessa felt heat flood her cheeks. She knew her face was likely beet red. Embarrassment tended to do that. The realtor hadn't even blinked when she'd made a mad dash past her with a muffled "excuse me" on her wild rush to the bathroom. Nice way to make a first impression.

They'd toured the whole cottage, viewed the two bedrooms, bathroom, and kitchen—and she loved everything about it.

"I really do want the place."

"I knew the moment we talked it would be perfect for you." Digging in her briefcase, Serena pulled out a sheaf of papers. With a flick of her wrist, she handed them to Tessa. "Here's the inventory sheet. It's best to get it filled out quickly, so Old Man Johnson doesn't have a conniption fit, and blame you for something you didn't do." Her grin was infectious, and Tessa found herself responding easily.

"I've got the first and last month's rent. Brought a money order, since I figured it might be easier until I can open a checking account locally. Sometimes out-of-state checks take a while, and I didn't want there to be any hang-ups." Reaching into her pocket, she pulled out the folded paper and handed it over. "You did get the deposit I wired, right?"

"Sure did. I'm so happy you decided to rent this cottage. I think it'll work great. The elementary school isn't far, so getting around shouldn't be a problem."

"I'm excited to get to know the students. I know I'm getting a late start for the upcoming year, with school beginning in a couple of weeks."

"Trust me, the school board was thrilled to get your application. They've been searching for a qualified replacement for Mrs. Edwards ever since she broke her hip and decided it was past time for her to retire. You're going to love it here."

Tessa ran her hand along the fireplace mantel, feeling the smooth texture of the polished wood against her fingers, and a little shiver ran up her spine. While the outside of the place might look worn down and neglected, the inside appeared perfectly charming. A fine coating of dust covered the floors, but would be easily remedied with a thorough cleaning.

Though the place wasn't huge, it was certainly big enough for one person, and she loved the hardwood floors and all of the character the older house brought. Plus having a second bedroom was an added bonus, allowing her to set up a separate office. "Can I ask you something?"

Serena cocked her head, a quizzical expression on her face. "Sure, ask me anything."

"Who was that guy? The one threatening to toss me in jail."

Serena laughed. "Rafe Boudreau. He's the sheriff. The Boudreaus are the nicest people in the world. Everyone loves them."

Tessa turned the information over in her head. Her heartbeat sped up when she thought about the tall, dark-eyed stranger. There had been—*something*—different about him. She couldn't put her finger on it, because she'd never felt anything like this instant connection before.

"Boudreau, huh? I'll have to remember the name."

Serena laughed harder, until tears shone in her eyes. "Take it from me. You'll get to know the Boudreaus intimately."

"Intimately?"

"I mean that in the nicest way. The Boudreaus are one of the oldest families in Shiloh Springs. They've been here for generations."

"Kind of like founding fathers of the community?"

"Exactly. They're not snooty like the Calloways. You won't meet kinder or more generous people. Another of the things you'll come to find out about living in Shiloh Springs. If you ever need anything, you ask Douglas or Ms. Patti. Heck, ask any of the Boudreaus and they'll give you the shirt off their backs." Serena gave her a conspiratorial wink. "And there are a lot of Boudreaus—most of them good-looking, single men."

Tessa barely refrained from rolling her eyes, watching Serena fan her face with one hand. "I'm not in the market for a guy, good-looking or otherwise. Since I'll only be here for one year, I plan to focus on the school year and learning new things about Texas."

"Your loss. If you change your mind, I'll be more than happy to introduce you to some of the eligible men here." Grabbing her briefcase, she headed for the front door. "Welcome to Shiloh Springs, Tessa. I have the feeling you're going to fit in here just fine."

With a quick wave, she left, and Tessa glanced around the living room. "I hope you're right, Serena, because for the next year, Shiloh Springs is my new home."

Early the next morning, Tessa stared at the meager pile of dishes she'd carefully stacked into the overhead cupboard. The small pile looked woefully inadequate in comparison to the vast emptiness on either side. Though the kitchen wasn't enormous, there were a lot of cabinets to fill.

Cutting open the next cardboard box to get out more stuff, she paused at the sound of the doorbell.

Great, company on my first day.

Brushing her hands on her jeans, she walked through the kitchen to the front door. A petite, older blonde woman stood on the porch. Definitely several inches shorter than her own five foot five, she looked like a stiff wind would blow her right off the porch, but the warmth of her smile instantly put Tessa at ease.

"Hello. You must be Tessa Maxwell. I'm Patricia Boudreau, and I wanted to welcome you to Shiloh Springs." Holding up a basket covered with a blue and white checkerboard-patterned cloth, the scent of freshly baked muffins tickled her nose. Tessa realized she'd been so caught up unloading the trailer, she hadn't stopped long enough to eat the night before, and her stomach chose that moment to rumble—loudly.

"Um, thank you. Please, come in."

Handing the basket to her, the other woman remarked, "Hope you like blueberry. I made a batch this morning for my oldest, and thought I'd drop by and say hi before I head over to his place." She leaned in, whispering, "He's probably still in bed."

A bit flustered, Tessa smiled. "I love blueberry."

Tessa skirted around the massive piece of furniture against the wall in the entryway. Standing over six feet tall and probably about as wide, it seemed like a combination coat rack, storage unit, antique mirror, and probably had a couple other functions she hadn't discovered yet. Near as she could figure, it looked like somebody cobbled together several pieces into one catch-all. One of her friends back in North Carolina loved going to garage sales and flea markets, and putting together what she lovingly called *Franken-*

furniture. This piece definitely fit the description. It was huge—and hideous.

She was grateful the place came with basic furniture, which meant she hadn't had to rent a full-sized moving truck, even if most of what came with the house wasn't exactly what she'd pick for herself. She led her guest across the entryway and into the kitchen.

"Sorry about the boxes. It was a long trip, and I kinda crashed once I got them unloaded last night." Moving aside a couple of the boxes, she made room at the cozy round table in the corner, flanked with windows on each side. Sunshine spilled through, highlighting the old wooden floors, the warm golden-brown patina showing signs of a few scratches, yet still giving the space a homey, comfortable, lived-in feeling. The kind of things that made a house feel like a home.

Patti Boudreau eased onto one of the chairs with the bearing of somebody comfortable in any situation, and hooked the straps of an oversized bag over the back of the chair. "I figured you'd probably be exhausted, hence the breakfast offering."

Realizing she still held the basket of muffins, Tessa placed them in the center of the table, before hustling over to the cabinet and taking down two small plates. Tiny blue flowers rimmed the edge, with a thin band of gold bordering the intricate floral design. She'd fallen in love with the dishes, a gift from her mother when she'd moved into her first apartment, and couldn't bear to leave them behind when she'd packed, though they were an extravagance. A wave of sadness filled her at the thought of her mother. It was hard to believe she'd never see her again. Straightening, she pushed aside the melancholy thought and smiled at her guest.

She handed one plate to the other woman, and sat in the chair opposite hers, reaching for one of the muffins. "Sorry I can't offer you coffee or anything. I haven't had a chance to head to the grocery store. I've been living on take out and Starbucks."

"Well, shoot." Mrs. Boudreau swiveled in her chair, and reached for the bag hooked over the chairback. She pulled out a large thermos and placed it on the table beside the basket of muffins. "I almost forgot, I brought coffee, too." She grinned, digging into her oversized bag again, and pulled out a couple of little containers of creamer and a handful of sugar packets. "Wasn't sure how you take yours, so I brought these."

"Mrs. Boudreau, you are officially my new best friend."

"Call me Ms. Patti, dear. Everybody does."

Pouring two cups, Tessa added creamer to hers and took a sip, then gave a blissful sigh. "You have no idea how much I needed that."

Ms. Patti chuckled. "Of course I do. I live in a house filled with men coming and going at all hours. Caffeine is one of the major food groups at our place." She took a sip and leaned back. "Now the niceties are over, tell me everything about yourself."

"Oh, boy, everything? There's not really much to tell. I heard about the teaching position, which came at a time I needed a change. The stars all aligned or something, because here I am."

Tessa wanted to squirm under the other woman's searching gaze. It felt like she was probing her very soul, before Ms. Patti finally picked up her cup again. "I'm sure there's more to you than meets the eye, but we've got all the time in the world to get to know each other better. But, remember, I'm here if you ever need anything. And I'm very good at keeping my mouth shut."

Tessa started to make an offhand remark, about not needing anything, but reading the sincerity in Ms. Patti's gaze, caught herself. It might be nice to have a friendly ear in this sea of unknown.

"Thank you, I appreciate it." She broke off a piece of the blueberry muffin and popped it into her mouth, savoring the sugary burst of flavor against her tongue, and couldn't bite back her moan of delight.

"Good?"

"Amazing."

Ms. Patti poured the rest of the coffee into Tessa's cup, and screwed the lid back on the thermos. "I understand you met my son yesterday."

Son?

Right. The tall, dark, and most-decidedly handsome man who'd left her tossing and turning half the night. His last name had been Boudreau.

"He caught me climbing through the front window. Thought I was a burglar."

Ms. Patti's brow rose at Tessa's words. "Really?"

Heat flooded her cheeks and she couldn't meet Ms. Patti's eyes. "Let's say it was a huge mistake to have an extra-large drink, followed by several hours in a car without stopping."

Understanding lit Ms. Patti's face along with a huge grin. "Ah, got it."

Tessa shrugged. "Fortunately, Serena showed up and saved the day."

"Serena's a lovely girl, and knows the area and the people. You have any questions or problems, don't hesitate to call her—or me."

"I appreciate it."

Ms. Patti stood, and tossed the thermos back into her oversized bag. "I've got someone scheduled to clean up the yard. They'll be here this afternoon."

"You don't have to do that."

"Nonsense. Should have been done before you moved in, but Old Man Johnson can be a bit...difficult."

"I'll need a referral for regular lawn care. Thought I'd ask Serena."

Ms. Patti chuckled. "Serena definitely has a list of repair

people for the area." She leaned toward Tessa and whispered, "I gave her a list. She's only been in Shiloh Springs about a year. Though I have to admit, she's become a wonderful asset to the community. Was she able to answer all your questions?"

Tessa nodded. "Absolutely."

"Good." Lifting the oversized bag, which seemed to dwarf her, Ms. Patti slung it over her shoulder and headed for the door. "Well, it's past time for my son to be up, so I'll be on my way. Now don't forget, you need anything, give me a call." Sliding her hand into the bag, she pulled out a business card and handed it over.

"I will. Thanks again for the breakfast and the coffee."

Stepping out onto the porch, she watched Ms. Patti climb behind the wheel of a white Cadillac Escalade and head down the street. Glancing at the card clutched in her hand, she noted the company name emblazon on the front. It was the company she'd rented the house from.

Beneath it were the words *Patricia Boudreau, broker.*

Tessa smiled, tapping the card against her palm. Serena wasn't kidding. The Boudreaus were everywhere.

CHAPTER THREE

Rafe peeled his eyeballs open, and groaned at the banging noise ricocheting around in his skull. When the sound repeated, he struggled to an upright position. Darn, he'd fallen asleep on the couch again, and the pounding noise was somebody banging on the front door.

"Just a second," he hollered, stretching to his full height, and felt the muscles in his lower back protest the movement. Picking up the remote, he muted the sound. Flinging open the door, he grinned at the sight of his momma standing on the front stoop.

At only five foot one, she barely reached the top of his shoulders, and looked like a fragile porcelain doll, something delicate and easily crushed, but he knew better. She might be petite, but she was fierce, whether it came to business or protecting her young'uns. A mama grizzly didn't hold a candle to Patti Boudreau.

"Don't tell me you fell asleep on the sofa again, son." She tilted her head back, and he brushed a kiss against her cheek, inhaling the scent of vanilla which seemed to accompany his momma wherever she went. "I don't care how many late night shifts you work, or how long the days are, there's a reason you have a bed in this house."

"I know, Momma." He shrugged. "Yesterday was one long day. I turned on the TV to catch the late news, and guess I crashed."

She chuckled and patted his cheek. "Your daddy did the same thing. He was still asleep when I left."

Brushing past him, she headed toward his kitchen, and he frantically tried to remember if he'd washed the batch of dirty dishes he'd had in the sink for the past two days.

"Rafael Felipe Alvarado Boudreau!"

Guess not.

Trailing behind her into the kitchen, he spotted her squeezing dish detergent into a sink rapidly filling with hot water and hung his head. He knew better, and usually kept a pretty decent house, but for the past couple of days the sheriff's department had been short-staffed. Summer colds had hit hard, and a good chunk of the staff had come down with the crud. He'd been overworked, exhausted to the bone, and let things slide. Trust his momma to show up before he had a chance to hide the evidence.

"I brought you breakfast," she said, plunging her hands into the mountain of bubbles, and attacking the plate she held, scrubbing hard enough he feared the pattern might come off. "Blueberry muffins. There's also fresh O.J. in the red thermos."

"Momma, you're a godsend. I'm starving."

"Son, you're always starving."

"I'm a growing boy," he mumbled around a mouthful of blueberry muffin. It was their running joke. She'd been telling him that for as long as he could remember.

Turning toward him, she winked. "Good thing you're an active boy, too, or you'd be broader than a barn." Rinsing her hands in the now-empty sink, she dried them on a kitchen towel, and leaned against the tiled counter. "I hear you met Tessa Maxwell last night."

Thinking about the pretty redhead, he couldn't stop the grin curving his lips. "I caught her climbing through a window at Old Man Johnson's place. I didn't know he'd decided to rent it. Thought she was a burglar."

His momma chuckled. "Like he'd have anything worth stealing in that old cottage. Nope. She's the new teacher."

Well, that certainly explained things. "How'd you know I met her? Serena?"

She shook her head. "I stopped by her place on the way over here, to welcome her to Shiloh Springs."

Which in Patti Boudreau speak meant she'd likely interrogated her mercilessly. Oh, his momma would have been the epitome of southern charm and hospitality, because that was simply her way, but he had no doubt she'd ferreted out each pertinent detail of Red's life in exquisite detail. There were days he wished he could hire her to come and interrogate suspects. They'd be confessing in no time.

"So, what'd you find out about Red? She tell you all her

secrets? Spill any juicy details?"

Ms. Patti's eyes narrowed, and he felt trapped, the proverbial deer caught in the headlights. *Tap, tap, tap.* Uh oh, whenever her foot began tapping on the tiled floor, he knew he was in trouble. From the moment he'd moved in with Douglas and Ms. Patti, back when he'd been nothing more than an angry, prepubescent, troubled boy, who through circumstances out of his control, ended up alone and homeless, he'd quickly learned his new mother was the sweetest woman on the face of the earth—until her toes started tapping—then it was best to stay under the radar and out of her line of fire.

"Now, Momma, I only meant..." He waved his hands, scrambling to figure out what set her off.

She chuckled, and patted his arm affectionately. "I'm just pulling your leg, son. Serena and I spoke yesterday, *before she went to meet Ms. Maxwell,*" she emphasized, "and I told her I'd stop by this morning. Give the poor woman a chance to settle in before the hordes descend." Walking to the sink, she picked up the towel she'd laid over the edge, neatly folded it, and placed it atop the countertop.

Reaching over, she ruffled his hair. "I know you're tired, but I'm recruiting my boys for a little work today. Finally got Old Man Johnson to agree to me fixing up the outside of the place."

"How'd you manage that?"

Her laughter filled the air. "Bribed him with free labor.

You know what a tightwad the man is. I simply made him an offer he couldn't refuse. Brody and Lucas are headed over there this afternoon."

"Lucas is home?" Last he'd heard his brother was in San Antonio, following up on a story he'd been investigating for weeks. One he hadn't gotten all the details on—yet—but if it was important or dangerous, his brother knew Rafe would have his back—always. If there was one thing the Boudreau brothers knew, family could always be depended on when you needed them.

"He got in a little past midnight."

"Glad he's home." He popped the last bite of muffin into his mouth and washed it down with the rest of the orange juice. "I'm off today, so I'll stop by this afternoon and help out. Least I can do, since I almost tossed your new tenant into a cell last night."

His momma grinned. Not her usual sweet grin. Nope, this was an I-know-something-you-don't-know grin. *And what the heck was that all about?* "She did mention it."

"Did she?"

Instead of answering, his mother gathered up the thermos and shoved it into her bag, pulling it up onto her shoulder.

"Momma—"

"I've got to run, I'm meeting a client in an hour." Reaching up, she brushed a soft kiss against his cheek, and he hugged her tight. Didn't matter what was happening in their lives, she never left without giving him a kiss goodbye. It was a lifeline he clung to, when everyday life seemed to get the better of him. Some days he'd stop by the ranch, just so he'd feel her soft lips against his cheek.

"Love you, son. I'll see you later."

"Love you too, Momma."

With a shrug, he headed for the shower. Since he was up and awake, he might as well get some work done before he headed over to Red's place.

CHAPTER FOUR

"Hello?"

"Tessa, you were supposed to call me when you arrived last night."

"Beth? Sorry. I barely had time to unload a couple of the boxes before I crashed."

"I may be a worrywart, but that's what big sisters do."

Tessa shook her head. Surely there had to be big sisters somewhere who didn't worry so much. Hers didn't happen to be one of them.

"Beth, we talked about this. I made a commitment to teach for a year in Shiloh Springs. Momma and Daddy wouldn't have wanted me to renege on my contract. They taught us better. Besides, after everything with Trevor, I needed a clean break. I thought you understood."

She heard Beth's sigh over the line. "I know. I can't believe how much I miss you already, though."

Tessa heard the underlying frustration in her sister's voice. Tessa had always been the good sister, the responsible one. Beth had been the frivolous one, the party girl, living life to its fullest, or at least she had until she'd gotten married. Now she was a stay-at-home mom with a husband and precious little Jamie.

Beth struggled with Tessa's decision to move to Texas, especially after the sudden death of their parents. Keeping her word and leaving her sister and her precious niece behind when all she wanted was the warmth of family was the hardest thing Tessa had ever done, but she knew beyond any doubt it was what her parents would have wanted.

Always the good daughter.

"Beth, I miss you, too. But the school year will go by fast, you'll see." She didn't want to tell her sister already some of the painful grief of losing her parents had lifted. Now instead of the overwhelming hurt and sorrow, she'd begun to feel a smidgeon of hope. Here in Texas, where her mother wasn't around every turn, it almost felt as if her mom and dad were back home, still alive, and waiting for her return.

"Well, I wish you hadn't taken a job so far away. I mean, Texas? Couldn't you have picked someplace closer?" The plaintive whine in Beth's voice caused her to smile.

"It won't be forever, Sis. I'm going to visit. And on the bright side, at least Trevor won't be following me all the way to Texas." Even he wasn't that crazy. *I hope.*

"I can't believe what a jackass he turned out to be. But enough about the jerk. What's it like there—Shiloh Springs? Have you met anybody yet?"

"I've actually met several people. They've all been very

nice." Well, except for the sheriff, who'd wanted to haul her to jail, but she was trying to forget about him. Forget about his dark chocolate-brown eyes. Forget his quirky grin. Forget about his wide shoulders, and how sexy he'd looked in his cowboy hat.

"Hey, you got awful quiet there, sis. Wait a second—did something happen you're not telling me?" Beth's voice got all high pitched with excitement. "You've been there less than twenty-four hours, and you've already met someone? Way to go, little sister!"

"It's not like that," Tessa protested, though knowing Beth, she wouldn't hear a word she said now. She'd be too busy marrying her off to a complete stranger. After all the trouble with her crazy ex, Trevor, Beth would be happy to see her date anyone, including Attila the Hun.

"Tell me all about him. What does he look like? Is he a cowboy? Was he riding a horse and wearing six shooters?"

"Seriously, Beth? Six shooters? What are you—twelve? I'm living in a rural but modern town, not out in the middle of West Texas cattle country. Besides, I met my *female* realtor yesterday, and one of the *female* local business people this morning." No need to mention said business person happened to be the good-looking sheriff's mother.

"Come on, let me live vicariously through you. I could stand to hear about somebody having a little romance in their life."

Uh oh, that didn't sound good.

"Sis?" She didn't want to broach the subject, but if Beth needed somebody to talk to…

"Everything's fine. I'm grumpy because Evan seems to work all the time—when he's not traveling. Jamie and I miss her daddy." Tessa heard Jamie squeal in the background at the sound of her name. A tiny fist squeezed the air out of her chest at the thought of her precocious niece. Just turned three, she was at an age where everything she did was adorable. Moving away from Jamie had been the hardest part of leaving.

"How is my princess?"

"She's been a holy terror all morning. I think she misses you."

"Not fair, Beth. Don't lay a guilt trip on me."

"Is it working? Because I'll put her on the phone if it'll make you come home."

Tessa chuckled. Beth would do it too. She wasn't above a little emotional blackmail to get her way.

"Give Jamie a kiss for me. I need to finish unloading the boxes, return the rental trailer, and finish unpacking."

"Fine. But I expect a call in a week. Promise?"

Rolling her eyes, Tessa gave her word. "Pinky swear. Now I really gotta go. Love you."

After a few more minutes of stalling, she finally hung up and glanced around at the still unpacked boxes, and decided a short mental break was called for before she dove back in. She grabbed her purse and keys, ready to head toward the center of Shiloh Springs. Yesterday, she hadn't taken the time, since she'd had an appointment to meet Serena, to do more than drive straight through the town.

First thing on today's to-do list—pick up some groceries and a coffee maker. She'd left her old one behind, since it was a relic and not worth packing.

Flinging open the door, she stared at the stranger standing on her porch, hand raised to knock. Hmm, Shiloh Springs certainly grew some mighty fine men. Standing several inches over six feet tall, with startlingly blue eyes, sandy brown hair, and the prerequisite cowboy hat shading his face, there was no denying he was attractive. Yet, he didn't send her stomach fluttering madly like Rafe Boudreau had.

"Morning, Ms. Maxwell." He touched the brim of his hat, his eyes twinkling. "I'm Brody Boudreau. My mother asked me to drop off a few things."

"I wasn't expecting anything."

He started to lean against the porch railing, but straightened when it shifted beneath his weight, a frown marring his otherwise handsome face. "It's not much. A few groceries and things to get you through until you can stock your cupboards."

"Oh, I was on my way to the grocery store, right after I return the rental trailer." She gestured toward her car. "It's very thoughtful of your mother, and I appreciate the gesture."

"Lemme grab the bags out of the truck. I'll be right back."

Her gaze followed him. She hadn't noticed the pickup truck parked at the curb, or the other man unloading yard equipment from the truck bed. From this far away, and with a hat obscuring his face, she couldn't tell much about him, except he was tall and whipcord lean.

Brody returned with several brown paper sacks, overflowing with food. "Want these in the kitchen?"

"Please."

Tessa pushed the front door open and stood back, watching him stride inside like he'd been there a thousand times before. Who knows, maybe he had. She followed behind, tossing her purse onto the countertop. Brody placed the bags on the table, and began unloading them. Fresh produce, eggs, cheese, meat, and bread. Far more than she'd have picked up on her own.

"This is too much."

He shot her a grin. "You'll have to take it up with Momma, because I'm not hauling it back out to the Big House."

The way he said the name definitely implied capital letters, and she repeated, "The Big House?"

"The Boudreau Homestead, known to the locals as the Big House, because the Boudreaus tend to have a houseful most of the time. Plus, it's the largest spread in the county." He continued unloading bags, placing the perishables into the refrigerator, like it was something he did every day. Which for all she knew, he might. Maybe he was the local grocer, and did this for a living. Although, she mused, giving him a long perusal, she didn't peg him for the indoor type.

The whirr of a lawnmower drifted through the open kitchen window, and it sounded really close. Like, in her yard close. Brody must have seen her confusion. "That'll be my brother, Lucas."

"Another Boudreau?"

He grinned. "You'll get used to it."

Shaking her head, she picked up the boxes of cereal and stowed them in the pantry, along with the canned goods Brody had lined up along the counter. She wasn't going to have to do any shopping for weeks, with all this food. Making a mental note to talk to Ms. Patti about reimbursing her, she heard a car door slam, and heavy footfalls against the wooden porch.

"Hey, Red, you here?"

Red? Nobody called her that, except…

"We're in the kitchen," Brody answered before she opened her mouth, and Rafe Boudreau strode into the space, instantly dominating the room. Funny how it hadn't seemed small until now.

"How's my favorite cat burglar this morning?" He gave her a wink, before giving a nod to his brother. Seeing them standing side by side, she couldn't spot any similarities between the two men. Different hair color, different eye color. Brody had an All-American look, while Rafe's appearance had a bit more exotic flare dark hair and deep brown eyes.

"Burglar? Looks like I missed out on all the fun."

Rafe grinned. "I'll let Red fill you in, if she wants. In the meantime, Momma stopped by this morning, and said you and Lucas planned to work on the outside of this place. Spruce things up. Figured I'd drop by and give you a hand."

"Guys, I appreciate the help, but…"

"No buts, Red. Momma's right. This place should have been ready inside and out by the time you arrived. It won't take us any time to put things to rights. You go ahead with whatever you were doing, and we'll be outside if you need anything." Rafe grabbed his brother's arm, and practically frogmarched him toward the front door.

"Nice meeting you, Ms. Maxwell," Brody called over his shoulder, shooting her a grin.

"Call me Tessa."

"She didn't say I could call her Tessa," she heard Rafe mutter, right before the front door closed behind the two men. A tiny smile touched her lips as she finished putting away the groceries, feeling a lightness inside she hadn't in a long time.

So far, she hadn't had a dull moment in Shiloh Springs. What else did this not-so-sleepy town have in store for her?

CHAPTER FIVE

"Okay, bro, what's the story with *Red*?" Brody grabbed a large pair of garden shears, and started clipping away at the overgrown bushes lining the front porch. Rafe set his toolbox on the first step, and bristled at the emphasis his brother put on the nickname he'd given Tessa, but let it slide. He didn't have any claim on the woman. Shoot, they'd just met the night before, yet he'd felt an instant chemistry with the feisty redhead. Had from the moment he spotted her climbing through the front window with her backside in the air.

"Not much to tell. Met her last night, right after she arrived. I simply kept her company until Serena got here." Which was the truth, minus the fun bits.

"Momma says she's the new teacher, taking over for Mrs. Edwards." Brody didn't look up from his work, so Rafe couldn't read his expression, but his interest in Red was evident.

"That's right."

"I sure don't remember having any teachers as pretty as her when I was in school. Might've paid more attention if I had."

Rafe didn't answer, watching Lucas make another sweep with the lawnmower. Even from a distance, Rafe noted the slight stoop to his brother's shoulders, the weariness in his stride. He couldn't help worrying about him. This latest story he'd been digging into was an ugly piece of work, and Lucas tended to get a little too personally involved in his investigations. While it made for some great exposés, it also left a deep scar on his psyche. He'd have to talk with him, see what he could do to help.

Opening the toolbox, he grabbed the hammer and a handful of nails, and went to work on the loose railing. Within minutes, the rickety spindles had been reattached, and the rail had lost its wobble. He stood back and surveyed his handwork, before adding a couple more nails to the front steps, making them more stable too.

A red Ford F-250 pulled up across the street, and Rafe grinned when his dad and his brother, Liam, stepped out. Looked like Momma had rallied the troops to take care of *Operation Fix Up the New Teacher's House*. Sending Douglas meant she expected things to run with military precision, because that's how his dad got things done. It was one of the many reasons he was in such high demand for construction jobs. He got things done right and on time.

"Hi, Dad. Come to check in, and make sure we're doing as ordered?"

"Your momma knows you boys won't let her down.

Now, get over here and help me with this stuff." Douglas pointed toward the back end of his truck. Liam was already busy unloading a ladder. Stepping closer, he spotted several buckets of paint and a couple of hand sanders.

Setting the paint buckets onto the porch, he spotted Tessa headed toward him with a tray in her hands. He reached for the screen door and held it open, and she stepped through, giving him a sheepish smile. Glancing down, he grinned and inhaled deeply. Though he wasn't sure how she'd managed it, in the short time he'd been outside, she'd whipped up a batch of cookies.

"I figured it was the least I could do, since you're all helping me."

"Well, I for one, appreciate it. I'll admit I've got a sweet tooth." Taking the tray from her hands, Rafe gestured toward the front, where the rest of his family made quick work of the landscape. The scent of freshly cut grass mixed with the fresh baked cookie smell, reminding him of weekends at the Big House, when he'd been a rowdy teenager.

"Hey, guys, take a break. Tessa made cookies."

The sound of the lawnmower cut off abruptly, and the other four men mounted the steps to the front porch. Tessa's eyes widened when she spotted his dad and Liam.

"Thanks, Tessa," Brody said with a grin, snatching two cookies off the plate. "Chocolate chip, my favorite."

Rafe moved a step closer and scowled at his brother, who

simply shrugged and stuffed half a cookie in his mouth.

"Red, this is my dad, Douglas Boudreau. The blond standing behind him is my brother, Liam, and the redhead is another brother, Lucas. Guys, this is Tessa Maxwell, the new teacher."

Douglas shot him a look before extending his hand. "Ms. Maxwell, it's a pleasure to meet you. Welcome to Shiloh Springs."

"Please, Mr. Boudreau, call me Tessa. And thank you all. This is…"

"A bit overwhelming?" Douglas chuckled, and scrubbed a hand across the back of his neck. "You can blame my wife. She started issuing orders the minute she got home, and assigned everybody jobs. Trust me, you don't say no to my wife."

"Good to know."

Finishing the cookies, the men went back to work, and Rafe followed Tessa into the kitchen. A half-empty bowl of cookie dough sat on the counter next to the oven. He bit back a grin when she began scooping out another batch of cookies onto a sheet tray and stuck them in the oven.

"Glad I made enough to do a second batch. I wasn't expecting so many people." She met his eyes, giving him a rueful smile. "Truthfully, I wasn't expecting any people. I'd planned on tackling a couple of things today, after I unpacked and returned the trailer. Which reminds me, I've still got to make it down there before they close."

"No problem. I'll drop it off for you."

"You don't have to do that."

"Gimme your keys and I'll run it over now, and be back before you know it. I know the guy who runs the place, and he won't mind staying open a few minutes. Especially when the sheriff asks nicely." His eyes twinkled as he added the last line, and she found herself smiling. "You can stay here and make a dent in those boxes."

He watched her nibble on her lower lip, worrying at it as she considered his offer. It was apparent she had no idea how adorable she looked, with her hair pulled back into a ponytail, her blue eyes sparkling. He could practically see her weighing her options in her head. Trust the sheriff with her car; don't trust a stranger with her car. Knew the exact moment when she made her decision.

Finally, with a shaky smile, she dug in her purse and pulled out her keys, handing them over along with the rental paperwork.

"I'll be back as fast as I can. If you think of anything else you need, have Dad or one of my brothers call me." With a wink, he strode out of the kitchen, tossing the keys into the air.

It was going to be a good day.

CHAPTER SIX

T essa straightened to her full height and stretched, her hands on the small of her back. She kicked aside the empty box she just unpacked. The Boudreaus had worked right up to sunset before heading home. The outside appearance of her new rental definitely showed improvement from the previous night.

The freshly mowed grass now spread across the front like a velvety blanket of green, and the overgrown and straggly bushes had been clipped and pruned until they looked lush and full, and exactly the right height to highlight the porch. The porch railing and steps were repaired too. The men had worked hard, only stopping for a quick lunch break before they went right back to it, accomplishing more than she'd imagined possible. All the chipped paint had been sanded smooth, though they hadn't gotten to actually paint anything. Douglas promised they'd be back the next day, after church, to finish the job.

Rafe returned her car, minus the trailer, about an hour after he'd left, but he'd been called in to the sheriff's office shortly thereafter, so she hadn't had a chance to thank him properly.

Picking up the empty box, she carried it to the back porch, where the other empty boxes were stacked. She needed to check with Ms. Patti in the morning, and find out about the city's recycling policy. She heard the slamming of a car door. A few seconds later, there was a knock.

Rafe stood on the other side. With a grin, he lifted up a picnic basket covered with a bright red cloth.

"I figured you'd probably be tired after all the hard work, so I brought dinner."

"Dinner? Honestly, I hadn't even thought about food."

"I'm not surprised. You've had a long day. It looks like the guys got a lot of stuff done after I left."

"I still can't believe everyone showed up and got through so much."

Rafe tilted back his cowboy hat and gave her a slow grin. "It's how we do things around here. You're in Texas now. We treat everybody like family."

Taking the basket from him, she led the way into the kitchen. Since the house didn't have a formal dining room, she'd been using the kitchen table for everything. Plus the space was cozy and warm, since she'd had the windows open most of the day. Warm? Who was she kidding? Texas in summer was downright stifling hot. Another point in the men's favor: they'd worked in the hottest part of the day without a single complaint.

Lifting the cloth off the top of the basket, her stomach

growled, and she realized it had been hours since she'd eaten.

"I wasn't sure what you'd like, so I grabbed some fried chicken and biscuits."

"Sounds great. Let me grab some plates. You are staying, right? I can't possibly eat all this by myself."

Rafe grinned, and she couldn't help noticing the twinkle in those deep chocolate-colored eyes. Again, there was a fluttering in the pit of her stomach, an awareness of how close he stood, and how much she liked looking at him.

"I was hoping you'd share."

Taking a deep breath, she took a deliberate step away, and reached into the cupboards, and lifted out plates and a couple of glasses. Fortunately, she'd made a fresh pitcher of tea earlier, and poured two glasses, filling them with ice. Rafe unloaded the basket's contents. He'd brought more than chicken and biscuits, she noted. Mashed potatoes and gravy and sweet corn filled plastic containers, and if she wasn't mistaken, there was an apple pie he'd snuck onto the countertop. It was her favorite, and she was sorely tempted to skip straight to dessert.

At the first bite, Tessa felt like she'd died and gone to heaven. Her feelings must have shown on her face, because Rafe chuckled.

"Everything's from Daisy's Diner on Main Street. Can't miss it. Just follow your nose, or the line of people. Best place to eat in Shiloh Springs."

"It's amazing." She took another bite, which was as delicious as the first, and glanced at Rafe, wondering why he'd come back. Was it really a friendly gesture, sharing dinner with a new neighbor, or was there something else behind his kindness?

"You've got a deer-caught-in-the-headlights look, Red. Afraid I'm going to break out the rubber hoses, maybe take you down to the station and interrogate you?"

"Am I that obvious?"

At his nod, she buried her face in her hands, and felt the heat rise in her cheeks. Darn it, she wished she didn't blush so easily, but being a redhead, it was a curse she'd borne since childhood. Still, she'd already made a memorial impression on him, and apparently things were headed from bad to worse.

"What do you want to know, Sheriff?"

"I'm off duty. Make it Rafe." There was that twinkle in his eyes again, a look of amusement on his face. "You don't have to tell me anything you don't want to, darlin'. But I'd like to get to know you better."

Drawing in a deep breath, she picked up her glass of tea and took a big drink. Her throat was suddenly as parched as the Sahara.

"I'm not used to being the new kid on the block. It almost feels like the first day of high school, where everybody knows everybody else, and you're standing at the front of the class trying to talk and nothing's coming out."

"Better than having the dream about showing up in

school naked."

"Not by much," she murmured, knowing her face was still red. "Okay, I'm twenty-eight. Born in a little town outside Charlotte, North Carolina. So small, you've probably never have heard of it. Went to college, got my teaching degree. That's about it."

His gaze was steady, and he studied her the whole time she spoke. She felt the intensity of his stare clear to her toes. It was like every ounce of his focus and concentration was centered on her, but not in a bad way. Like he really wanted to know about her. She definitely wasn't used to being the object of attention, even in a room with only the two of them.

"I'm sure there's a whole lot more to you, Red, but it'll do *for now.*"

A tingle raced across her skin at his last words. Did that mean he planned to spend more time with her? "I've really led a very boring life, Sheriff. Nothing notable or remarkable about me."

"I have to respectfully disagree, Red. From what I've seen, you are exceptionally remarkable—and memorable."

Okay, then. It was hard, but she resisted the urge to fan her face. She couldn't help wondering if he felt the same pull, the instant connection she'd felt from the moment she'd met him. Unsure, she decided a change of subject was in order.

"Tell me about your family. Serena said there are a lot of

Boudreaus around?"

At her question, Rafe tilted his head back and laughed, and she watched the muscles in his throat move. He wiped at his eyes, as the last peals of laughter subsided. "Truer words have never been spoken. There are most definitely a lot of Boudreaus in Shiloh Springs." He lifted his tea and took a long swallow. "You've met Douglas and Patricia, my parents. Plus Brody, Lucas, and Liam. Then there's Antonio, Heath, Shiloh, Ridge, Chance, Joshua and Dane. And we can't forget Veronica, Nica to her friends. She's pretty much the pampered princess of the family."

"That's...a lot of Boudreaus."

"Which comes with some very interesting history. Stick around long enough, and maybe I'll share all the details with you."

She knew she was gawking, but she couldn't help it. Though he'd spoken with affection about his siblings, there was also something else underlying his words, a fierce wealth of emotion with each name spoken. There wasn't any doubt he loved his family.

Standing, she picked up his plate and hers, and headed toward the sink. "You brought dinner, I'll take care of the dishes. Did I say thank you for the food? And the company?"

He leaned his hip against the counter. "I'm glad you enjoyed it. I should probably head out, let you get some rest. See you tomorrow at church. Afterwards, we'll get the painting done." Taking a step forward, his hand cupped her cheek and her breath caught. Without thought, she found herself leaning into his touch. His thumb slid across her lips in the softest, gentlest caress, before he slowly lowered his hand and stepped back, his expression guarded.

"Goodnight, Red."

"'Night, Sheriff."

Without a backward glance, he walked out and she heard his engine start. Seconds later, he was gone, leaving her enveloped in silence. Leaning against the kitchen wall, her fingertips pressed against her lips, and she could still feel the warmth of his touch.

Don't be an idiot, Tessa. He's being a good neighbor. Don't read more into his actions than he meant.

With a shake of her head, she pulled out storage bowls and put away the remaining food, turned off the light, and headed for bed. She had the feeling her dreams would be filled with a tall, dark, and definitely sexy sheriff.

CHAPTER SEVEN

A few days later, Rafe pulled his car into the elementary school parking lot. He didn't have any official business here. Heck, he should be heading down to the McAllister place to ask Joel McAllister a few questions about his whereabouts the night before. Instead, he turned his car into the faculty lot and parked alongside Tessa's.

He hadn't seen her since Saturday night, when he'd brought dinner by her place. The office had been short-staffed with the summer cold everybody seemed to be passing back and forth, and he'd worked double shifts the last few days. Staying away from Tessa had been harder than he'd anticipated, but fortunately the job kept him busy, and kept his mind off the pretty redhead, at least while he was awake. His dreams, on the other hand…

I won't stay long. This is strictly a follow-up, to make sure she's settling in without problems.

Funny how he didn't believe his own thoughts.

He knew precisely where he'd find her. Mrs. Edwards' classroom was halfway down the central corridor, on the right. The same classroom where she'd taught when he'd been in this very same school, though he hadn't been in her class.

The first thing he spotted through the open doorway was Tessa, bent over a cardboard box. He bit his cheek to hide the grin threatening to spread across his face. Seemed like every time he saw her, she had her outstanding backside on display. Realizing he was staring, he cleared his throat, drawing her attention.

"Rafe! I didn't see you there."

"I wanted to stop by and make sure you're settling in with no problems." He glanced around the classroom, noting the changes. The blackboard and desk still sat regally at the front of the classroom, one side of the blackboard lined with permanent lines for teaching the little ones to write their letters and numbers. The other half was enticingly blank. Three windows ran along the right side, providing a perfect view of the outdoors, with swings and monkey bars and lots of green grass. In a few weeks, the sound of children's laughter and squeals of delight would fill the air, because recess was usually a big part of the day—at least that's how he remembered second grade. Some things never change.

"Things have been great. The principal got me up-to-date on Mrs. Edwards' incoming students, the curriculum, and has made me feel welcome." The tiny smile accompanying her words evoked a deep warmth inside him. An unfamiliar sensation, but not an unwelcome one.

"Good. Any problems settling in otherwise?"

Sheesh, Boudreau, you're really killing it with the small talk. Get a grip, man.

"The house is great. I'm pretty much unpacked and got everything put away. Please thank your family again for all their help. And thank you too. The outside of the place looks amazing. Quite the transformation."

His hand rubbed the back of his neck at her praise. "I'll tell them."

There was a moment of silence, before Tessa turned back toward her unpacking. "I know there's a few weeks before school starts, but I'm really excited. Interacting with the kids will make things seem...I don't know...more real." She chuckled. "I still have trouble believing I packed up my stuff and moved halfway across the country for a job."

"I'm glad you did."

He really should get going before Joel McAllister high-tailed it to the creek, where the teenagers congregated during the hotter days of summer. With school out, most of them spent these lazy sunny afternoons swimming or fishing, and sometimes doing other things teenagers do, which was one of the reasons he needed to speak with the young man. Apparently, Joel had been canoodling with one of the young ladies, and her parents were unhappy and threatening to press charges.

Yet, he was oddly reluctant to leave Tessa's side.

"How'd you hear about the job here—in Shiloh Springs, I mean? We're not exactly at the top of most people's top ten places to relocate."

She lowered the handful of books she'd taken from the box, setting them onto the corner of the desk. "Jill Monroe mentioned the position." His surprise at the mention of Jill's name must have shown, because she quickly continued. "Jill and I went to school together, shared a few classes. We've kept in touch on and off since then. When it was determined Mrs. Edwards would be laid up for several months with her broken hip, she thought about me. I know she discussed it with the principal before calling and asking if I'd be interested."

"Obviously you were, or you wouldn't be here."

She gave a sharp nod. "Honestly, I've been at loose ends for a while. My parents passed away a couple of months ago. It was unexpected, and hit me hard. Other than my sister, Beth, and her daughter, they were all the family I had."

"I'm sorry for your loss, Red." Placing a hand on her shoulder, he squeezed gently, and felt her sigh.

"Thank you. Beth has her husband and her daughter to lean on, which makes it easier for her. At least I hope so. I feel like I've been floundering, without an anchor to hold me in place. When Jill called, and then Mr. Sanchez, with the job offer, it seemed like an omen. A year away from North Carolina, away from every sight and sound that evoked their memories and the loss, seemed like an excellent idea."

Her grief was like a palpable blow, and he hated imagining her dealing with the loss of not one, but both parents. A feeling he was all too familiar with. His natural curiosity made him wonder how they'd died, but even he wasn't insensitive enough to ask.

"Well, I'm sure the parents of Shiloh Springs' students are grateful you've stepped in. If you need anything, don't hesitate to ask." Picking up the hat he'd tossed on the desktop earlier, he started for the doorway, but pulled up short, remembering why he'd dropped by.

"We're having a barbecue at the Big House on Saturday, and Momma wants you there."

"The Big House, that's your family's home, right?"

"The Boudreau family homestead. The place has been in the family for generations. Used to be a much larger working ranch, but we've cut back on the number of head we're running now. Dane always wanted to carry on the family's cattle ranching tradition, but the rest of my brothers all went into different jobs. Everybody lends a hand when they can, though."

While he'd been talking, Tessa stood beside the desk, and a shaft of sunlight through the window played across her skin, making her appear to glow. The deeper red highlights in her hair shone like fire bursts, little flames flickering to expose the hidden embers. There was no denying her appeal, and the pull he felt toward her was unlike anything he'd felt before. The thought of pursuing this elusive feeling both intrigued and terrified him.

Turning toward him, she smiled. "Can I ask a nosy question?"

"Sure."

"Your brothers, the ones who came to my house? You all look so different." He watched a wash of pink flood her cheeks. "I mean different hair color, different eye color. And none of you look like your mother or father."

He chuckled at her perplexed expression. She wasn't the first person who'd been confused about his family. "Tell you what, Red. You agree to come to the barbecue with me on Saturday, and I'll tell you the whole story. Deal?"

"How can I refuse an offer like that, Sheriff?"

His lips twitched into a smile. "I'm hoping you can't. Don't forget, give me a call if you need anything—anything at all. And I'll pick you up at eleven Saturday morning."

"I can—"

"See ya, Red."

Without another word, he turned and walked toward his car, already looking forward to Saturday. Until then, though, he needed to talk to Joel McAllister and put the fear of jail into him.

CHAPTER EIGHT

Pouring a glass of iced tea, Tessa walked into the second bedroom, the one she'd converted into an office. The space wasn't huge, probably ten by twelve, but it was more than enough to house a desk, printer stand, file cabinet and bookcase. Plopping down onto the floor by the last boxes waiting to be unpacked, she ripped the tape free, and flipped open the lid.

Notebooks filled with teaching materials she'd collected over the past few years, both from classes she'd taught, as well as from other teachers, lined the inside. Things she used as inspirations for lesson plans, and things to pique the children's interest, lay beneath. Pulling them out, she stacked them on the bottom shelf of the bookcase, before reaching inside the box for more.

When her hand wrapped around a leather-bound book, she paused as memories spilled through her. How did it get in there? Her forehead crinkled as she wracked her brain, trying to remember, because she could've sworn she'd packed it in one of the boxes Beth was holding for her back home.

This book was one of her most prized possessions. Her

great-grandmother's recipe book, passed down from her great-grandmother, to her gran, and then her mother. Now it was hers, because Beth hadn't wanted it. While her sister loved the recipes they'd eaten as kids, after she'd gotten married it had become a well-established fact that she couldn't cook. At all. Even making toast surpassed her limited culinary skills.

But Tessa loved cooking, and making those old family recipes filled her with joy. Lovingly, she ran her hand across the embossed front, felt the supple leather, the worn places where hands had held it through four generations of women. Pulling it to her chest, she closed her eyes and inhaled the scent of aged leather and paper. With a shuddering breath, she willed away the tears threatening to fall. Oh, the meals her mother made using these recipes handed down through the years. Old Southern classics, the kind of things you didn't find in fancy restaurants, but good, hearty, stick-to-your-ribs meals.

"Mom, I miss you so much."

A feeling of warmth suffused her, and she clutched the book tighter, before laying it across her lap and opening the front cover. Looking at the first page, she saw her great-grandmother's handwriting, neat and precise, and perfectly legible even all these years later. The instructions for a dash of this or a pinch of that made her smile.

"I promise, I'll take very good care of this. Someday it'll be passed along to my daughter or Jamie. I won't let the love and care of these recipes be forgotten."

She flipped through the next few pages, finding little loose pieces of paper stuck between pages. Sometimes there were measurements written down in a spidery script. Sometimes it was an ingredient list. Receipts from the nineteen fifties. Even a grocery list from her grandmother for her mother's sixth birthday party. The emotions and memories overwhelmed her, and she placed the book on top of the bookcase. It was a good spot for now, though she had no doubt it would end up in the kitchen eventually, once she'd fully settled in.

Emptying out the rest of the box's contents, she pulled the last one in front of her. Before she could peel back the tape, a knock sounded on her front door.

"Just a minute, I'm coming," she yelled, rising from the floor in a not-so-graceful stumble. She rushed toward the door and pulled it open, grinning when she saw who stood on the other side.

"Jill! Come in, come in. I'm so happy to see you!"

Her friend gave her a hug, and walked into the living room. "The place looks great. I noticed fresh paint on the porch and shutters too. You have been busy."

"I can't take the credit for the changes. The Boudreaus are responsible for sprucing up the outside. They showed up Saturday morning, and before I knew it, they'd pretty much taken over."

Jill shook her head, chuckling. "Girlfriend, you're going

to find the Boudreaus will steamroll right over you if you're not careful. If Ms. Patti takes you under her wing, you'll probably never have to lift a finger again. Seriously, the woman is a miracle worker."

"Well, they certainly worked miracles here. Now, tell me everything going on with you."

"Not much to tell."

"Wait, I thought you were dating what's his name, Walt, Wilt…"

"Ugh, don't remind me. Walt and I are kaput. Finito. Splitsville. As in, the lousy, cheating, good-for-nothing louse better never show his face around me again, or I will not be responsible for my actions. He's been lying to me the whole time, and I probably wouldn't have found out if his *wife* hadn't found my number in his phone."

"Wife?" Tessa reached over and grabbed Jill's hand, squeezing tight. "He was married?"

"I do not date married men—ever. And the lying scum knew it too. Probably why he didn't tell me. I even asked around before I agreed to date him, and nobody said a word. Of course, he doesn't live in Shiloh Springs, so they might not have known, but still…"

"Tell me where he lives and I'll make him sorry he ever messed with Jill Monroe."

"Don't worry, I think the soon-to-be ex Mrs. Walt can handle things with the lying scumbag. Besides, he's made his bed and now he can suffer the consequences of being a cheating hound dog." Flinging herself down on the sofa, Jill curled one leg beneath her, and patted the cushion beside her. "Never mind about me. Tell me what happened with Trevor."

Tessa bit back the curse which immediately sprang to her lips. "Trevor wasn't any better than Walt—except he wasn't married. Things got really, I don't know, creepy. He was always around, even when we didn't have a date. Showed up at my house. Heck, he even showed up at my job. And the phone calls. Constantly checking up on me, needing to know where I was every minute of the day. It finally got too much, and I dumped him."

"Good riddance, I say."

Tessa didn't say anything else, because she hoped her past would stay back in North Carolina, and she'd use this year to put some time and space between her and Trevor St. James. Much needed time, because after the breakup, he'd gotten even worse. She'd changed her phone number, yet he somehow managed to get it and the calls didn't stop. As a last resort, she'd taken out a restraining order against him, stating he wasn't allowed within a hundred feet of her. It worked—for a while. She'd gotten a few months respite. Now she was in Texas, maybe he'd finally get the message and let things go.

Jill laid her head on Tessa's shoulder and gave a loud sigh. "Feels like we're back in college, doesn't it? How many times did we lean on each other, help each other through the line of losers we seemed to attract?"

Tessa gave an exaggerated shudder. "More than I care to remember."

"Does it ever get easier?"

"Are you sure I'm the right person to ask? I'm still single too, and haven't dated in longer than I care to remember." Tessa nudged Jill's leg aside and stood, headed for the kitchen. "I don't have anything stronger than iced tea. Want some?"

"Sure. Don't suppose you've got any ice cream to go with it?"

Setting the filled glasses on a tray, she took down two bowls and filled them with the fudge ripple ice cream she'd picked up the day before. Adding spoons to the tray, she headed back to the living room, and set the tray on the coffee table.

"Here you go. Dig in."

Jill grabbed the bowl and shoved a heaping spoonful into her mouth, leaning back against the cushions with a contented sigh. "Thanks, I needed that."

When they'd finished the ice cream, Tessa turned to her friend. "You still working for that insurance company?"

Jill rolled her eyes before nodding. "Unfortunately. I'm beginning to think I'm going to be answering phones and writing policies when I'm ninety."

Tessa knew how much her friend hated her job. She'd bemoaned the fact unless she moved to a bigger city, she was stuck with a dead-end job without any prospect of advancement. "I only wish there was some way you could follow your dream."

"Not much chance of that happening, girlfriend."

"You are still baking, aren't you?"

"Sure. I love it, even if there isn't much call for anything more than a birthday cake every now and then. I only do them for my friends, you know?"

"Girlfriend, I remember some of the creations you whipped up in your spare time. I've never seen anything like them—or tasted any better. Why haven't you considered opening up a shop?"

Jill nibbled on the edge of her nail before reaching for her phone. "I think about it every day. I know exactly how I'd set it up, what I'd offer. But starting a business takes money, and working at an insurance company isn't exactly bringing in the big bucks." She scrolled through some photos on her phone before handing it to Tessa.

The photo on the screen displayed the most beautiful cake Tessa had ever seen. An exquisite confectionary masterpiece, it stood four tiers high, and was covered with a pattern of flowers and lace, the intricate delicacy of each bloom a work of art in itself. The vivid colors along with the detailed exotic blooms made the cake seem like a three-dimensional sculpture.

"Jill, it's stunning." She touched the screen, enlarging a close-up of one of the blooms. "The details—you'd swear these were real."

"Yeah, I'm kinda proud of that one. I spent days getting every detail right."

"Tell me you sold it for some really special occasion."

Jill hung her head, refusing to meet Tessa's gaze. "I told you, I make the occasional birthday cake, nothing special."

Tessa's gaze shifted between her friend and the photo on the screen. Playing a hunch, she slid her finger on the phone, and pulled up the next photo. Another cake displayed, this one a sheet cake with a tropical beach scene, complete with palm trees and a vibrant sunset. Each sweep of color made the waves washing against the shore come to life, the seashells decorating the border fragile and unique.

"These should be gracing the pages of cooking magazines. They're exquisite." Her hand moved again, and picture after picture showed delectable confections—cupcakes, macarons, and eclairs—each one the picture of perfection. With reluctance, she handed back the phone, wishing there was something she could do or say to help Jill fulfill her dream. She'd been baking ever since Tessa met her. Heck, in school she'd kept them supplied with enough cookies and pastries to last through binge-worthy stretches of studying.

"It's a pipe dream. Maybe someday, who knows?" Jill sat up straighter and reached for her tea. "Enough Melancholy Nelly. Tell me how things have been since you got to Shiloh Springs." She waved a hand toward the front door. "You've obviously met the Boudreaus." The grin accompanying her words was infectious, and Tessa found herself responding.

"From what I understand, I've met some of the Boudreaus. Apparently, there are a few more, but I've been invited out to their home on Saturday. Guess I'll meet the rest of them then."

"Lucky you. Which ones have you met?"

"Hmm. Douglas and Ms. Patti." She paused, letting the silence draw out, knowing Jill wouldn't let her get away without telling her every little detail. Though she probably wouldn't mention exactly how she'd met her first Boudreau.

"And..."

"Let's see. Brody. And Lucas. Oh, and Liam."

If she hadn't been watching Jill's face closely, she probably wouldn't have noticed the slight wince at the mention of Lucas' name, though she quickly disguised it. Not quick enough, though. There was a story there, and Tessa would find out—but not now. She was just getting over the whole Walt fiasco, might not be a good idea to open any old wounds.

"I think you left somebody off your list, girlfriend."

Trust Jill to notice.

"You mean our esteemed sheriff?"

"A little birdy told me the two of you met your first night in town. Interesting how you neglected to mention it."

Tessa scrunched her brow, trying to figure out how Jill knew. Who in the world could have told...

"You know Serena." It wasn't a question.

Jill giggled. "She mentioned you and the sheriff looked decidedly chummy when she pulled into the drive."

There was no way she was telling Jill about what happened, and how Rafe threatened her with jail. Giving her friend that kind of ammunition? She'd never hear the end of it.

"It was nothing. He saw me waiting on the porch, and stopped by to make sure everything was alright. That's it."

"Hmm, why do I get the feeling there's more to the story than you're telling?"

"Because you've got a twisted imagination? Seriously, Jill, I barely know the man."

Her friend suddenly sat up straighter. "Now, I know something happened. Look at your guilty face. Come on, spill."

"Seriously, nothing happened." When Jill crossed her arms over her chest and gave her a mulish expression, she gave in. "Fine. He did stop by Saturday night and brought dinner, but nothing happened, I swear."

Jill settled back against the cushions, a dreamy expression on her face. "Dinner with Rafe Boudreau. The two of you, all alone, no prying eyes watching your every move? Was it romantic?"

"No! He was simply being neighborly. We talked, we ate. End of story."

Except when he touched my lips, and looked into my eyes.

That certainly felt more than neighborly. It felt—magical.

"Well, shoot. I was hoping for some excitement, maybe a few sparks. I could live vicariously through you, since I'm obviously not jumping back into the dating pool anytime soon."

"We'll commiserate together. In the meantime, we'll eat more ice cream."

"Sounds good, except I've gotta run. Have I told you how happy I am you're here in Shiloh Springs?"

"Maybe once or twice," Tessa grinned, hugging her friend. "Let's make plans to have dinner next week. Really spend some time catching up."

"It's a plan. I'll call you."

Tessa walked her to the door, and stood on the front porch until the taillights faded from sight. Seeing Jill, reconnecting with her friend, felt good. Gave her a bit of an anchor to Shiloh Springs, and helped her feel settled. Not that she hadn't been welcomed by the people she'd met—to the contrary, everyone seemed thrilled she was covering for their beloved Mrs. Edwards. But being the new kid on the block was an odd feeling for her.

Turning off the porch light, and locking the door, she headed back for the office to unpack the final box.

CHAPTER NINE

Saturday morning dawned way too early, and Rafe was up to meet the sunrise after a sleepless night. It had been a long shift, with two deputies out sick, leaving the sheriff's office shorthanded again. The night seemed endless, filled with domestic disturbance calls, one drunk and disorderly charge, and somebody firing potshots at Old Man Grady's barn. Nobody got hurt, but Grady had been fit to be tied, swearing he'd hunt down the varmints and blast 'em full of buckshot. It took a bit of fast talking to keep Grady from heading out with his shotgun, hellbent on dishing out his own brand of justice.

Maybe he could blame it on the full moon, but everybody seemed extra loco, and a few folks ventured into plain old stupid.

The topper of the night? Eliza Boatwright, driving her husband's beat-up John Deere into the center of town, belting out *Jolene* at the top of her lungs while driving down Main Street. Off key, and loud enough the ole coon hound of Marcus Givens took to howling right along with her. Of course, she'd been wearing a see-through nightie with nothing underneath at the time. Reeking of Dennis' homemade moonshine, which tended to get stronger with each batch, she'd been three sheets to the wind. Since Dennis Boatwright wasn't in any better shape to drive into town and claim his wayward bride, Rafe ended up calling in reinforcements, otherwise known as his momma, to help sober up Eliza before sending her home to sleep it off. Another fun night at the Shiloh Springs Sheriff's office.

He'd returned home exhausted around five a.m. and fallen into bed, barely able to keep his eyes open, sure he'd sleep for hours. Instead, he'd tossed and turned, unable to keep his mind off the pretty redhead he'd be taking out to the family homestead later that morning. Tessa Maxwell was quickly making herself a part of Shiloh Springs, weaving her way into the hearts of the parents and their kids.

She'd gotten a list of students for the upcoming semester, and was methodically and efficiently working her way through it, introducing herself to each family, and letting them get to know her and her plans for the class, letting the parents ask her questions about her background and her qualifications. Seemed like a great way to both get to know the community up close and personal, as well as let people know she wasn't some stranger who'd come to brainwash their children with all sorts of newfangled teaching ideas. It felt great to have such a conscientious teacher becoming part of Shiloh Springs.

He also remembered his promise to tell her about his

family. Shaking his head, he picked up his coffee. Everybody around Shiloh Springs knew about his past. It wasn't a secret. He didn't try and hide away from the harsh truth of his early years, but he didn't go around gossiping to every Tom, Dick, and Harry who came along either. There wasn't a thing he wouldn't do for Patti and Douglas Boudreau—nothing. And he was pretty sure his brothers felt the same. Every one of them would lay down their lives for the couple who'd raised them. Loved them. Taught them right from wrong, and took them in when their worlds crumbled around them. Scared boys who didn't know where to turn or who to trust. They'd been at their most vulnerable, lowest point, and Patti and Douglas had been the bright light in their darkness.

Glancing at the clock, he grimaced at the time. Barely eight, and he wasn't picking Tessa up until eleven. Trying to fall back asleep was useless. He'd given up on getting any. Instead, he slid his feet into the sneakers by the kitchen door, and headed to the back of the house, straight for the shed. *Might as well get a couple of hours in, while it's still cool outside.* Cool by Texas standards anyway. It wasn't unusual for morning temps to already be in the upper seventies at daybreak, and easily reach triple digits by late afternoon. That was without factoring in the heat index, which made it feel like you were standing inside a kiln having your skin baked off.

He hefted a bag of mulch and tossed it into a wheelbarrow, followed by another. A bag of fertilizer joined them, and he guided the whole thing around to the side of the house. Every spare moment, he worked his way around the perimeter of the house, and things were finally taking shape. The height of summer wasn't the best time of year for planting, but he kept soaker hoses dripping to beat the drought. They kept the earth damp, and made the greenery lush and the flowering plants bloomed well past when most everybody else's died back.

Ms. Patti had been the first person who discovered his affinity with plants. As a scared, snot-nosed kid, he'd been terrified out of his mind at the rapid changes unfolding in his life. First, he'd been forced to move in with a new family. His entire life imploded around him, ended in shambles, and he'd wound up alone and frightened. The night his world fell apart, Douglas Boudreau arrived like a superhero, the kind he read about in his friends' comic books. The bigger-than-life man swooped in and claimed Rafe, giving him not only a home, but a refuge, a personal port in the midst of chaos. More importantly, though, he given him the one thing he'd never had in his entire life—a loving family.

A couple of days after coming to live with the Boudreaus, Ms. Patti took him to her secret place—her hidden garden. She'd showed him the differences between the healthy growing plants and the strangling weeds which threatened their lives. She never once complained when he came inside covered with dirt and mud. She'd simply hug him and praise his efforts, and thank him for helping with her garden. Together, they spent hours under the hot sun, fingers in the rich black soil, and he'd learned to love making things grow.

Dropping to his knees, he pulled a few weeds, the nasty little buggers who'd managed to get past the protective membrane, and tossed them into a small pile at his side. It felt good to sink his fingers into the rich dark dirt. Rising, he picked up the first bag of mulch, and glanced toward the street as a black pickup truck pulled into his drive. His sister, Nica, jumped from the passenger seat and raced across the grass, her long blonde hair flying behind her.

"Rafe!"

"Hey, short stuff, when'd you get into town?" Her arms wrapped around him in a hug, and he squeezed back, careful not to let his dirt-encrusted hands touch her. She'd been away at college much of the summer, taking extra classes. Nobody had told him she'd be home this weekend.

"I decided to surprise Momma and Dad. Took a few days off. I miss everybody."

He nodded to his brother, Joshua, who'd apparently been recruited as chauffeur for their sister. Veronica, or Nica to her family, was the lone girl in the Boudreau clan. They teased her about being the pampered princess, though nothing could be further from the truth. Growing up with a house full of brothers, she'd learned to roughhouse and keep up with the boys, but since heading off to school, she'd gained a bit of feminine grace and polish. Yet deep down, she was still Nica, the baby sister he'd rocked to sleep more times than he could count.

"Made it in time for the barbecue. Why am I not surprised?"

She grinned. "Another reason I made the trip home. Everybody except Ridge and Shiloh are gonna be there, at least that's what Momma said when I talked to her last week. I can't wait to see Antonio and Heath. It seems like forever since we were all together."

"Heath's coming?" *Wonder why nobody mentioned that, either? When did I fall out of the loop?* Heath worked with the ATF, and he'd been offered a big chance at advancement if he'd relocate to the nation's capital. Of course, he'd jumped at the chance, packed up and moved to Arlington, Virginia, and commuted to D.C. He hadn't seen his brother in over a year.

Nica bounced on her heels beside him, filled with youthful exuberance. He smiled, remembering how she'd always been the hardest to pin down and keep still. Constantly moving, always on the go. "I had lunch with Antonio last week, and he said he was planning to drive down if he could get the time off. I couldn't pass up the opportunity to see everybody, so I convinced Joshua to pick me up."

"And she talked my ear off the entire way. Wouldn't even let me turn on the radio." His brother leaned against the corner of the house, his cowboy hat shading his face. "Figured I'd drop her off here, so I could get five minutes of blessed silence."

"Hush up. I do not talk too much," Nica scolded, hands on her hips and a scowl on her face.

Rafe met his brother's eyes, and burst into laughter. The family teased Nica endlessly because she was a well-known chatterer. On any subject. At any time. Mention a topic, and she was off to the races. The girl did love to talk.

Sinking to her knees, she tugged a couple errant weeds he'd missed, and tossed them onto the bedraggled pile. "This looks really great, Rafe. You've gotten a lot done since the last time I was here." She pointed to the two gardenia bushes he'd planted earlier in the spring. The white blooms gave off the strong fragrance he liked, so he'd placed them beneath his bedroom window, directly under the painted shutters. In the late evenings, he left the window open, allowing him to catch subtle whiffs of their sweet fragrance all night long.

"It's coming along pretty good. I planned on getting some mulch down, wanna help?" His gaze shifted between Nica and Joshua.

"No can do, big brother. I promised Momma I'd be back to help get stuff ready for the get together, but I couldn't wait to see you." A grin formed on her lips. "Besides, from what I heard, there might be a certain somebody new in your life. I wanted to hear it from the source."

It took him a second to realize she was talking about Tessa. Who in the world...he looked at Joshua, who simply shrugged. No help there.

"Get her outta my hair, Josh. I've got work to do if I'm going to make it to the Big House on time." Reaching down, he gripped Nica's elbow, and pulled her to her feet.

"But, you haven't told me about—"

He touched one dirt-stained finger to the tip of her nose. "Curiosity killed the cat, kiddo."

"A, I am not a cat. B, you might as well tell me. You know I'm gonna find out anyway. And C, I can have Josh drive me over to her house and get all the dirt straight from the horse's mouth." Standing there with a self-satisfied smirk, hands on her hips, he realized she probably would. There wasn't a bashful bone in his baby sister's body. Sighing, he wrapped his arm around her shoulder, and steered her toward the truck.

"Her name is Tessa Maxwell. She's the new grade school teacher. There isn't anything to tell, because we haven't been out. I've been too busy, and she's getting ready for school to start."

He almost laughed out loud at the disappointed expression on Nica's face. "Really? Not even one date? You're not getting any younger, you know." Going on her tiptoes, she brushed a kiss against his cheek. "Besides, I worry about you. You're my big brother and I love you. I want you to be happy."

"I am happy, squirt." Watching her climb onto the passenger seat, he closed the door, and leaned in to whisper. "I'm bringing her to the barbecue, so you'll get to meet her.

But," he paused, when she started doing a little booty shake in her seat, "give her a break. Don't pull any of your interrogation tactics on her. Got it?"

Nica grinned. "Got it. See you later, alligator."

"After a while, crocodile."

At the sound of her joyous laughter, he joined in. She'd been saying that since she was three, and heaven help you if you didn't answer her with the next line. Seeing her happy and smiling lifted his spirits. His baby sis was a gift from God, and though they might not be blood, he loved her as if she was—because she was family.

And family means everything.

He glanced at Joshua. "Get her outta here. I've got to finish the mulch and grab a shower. See you later."

It wasn't until the pickup truck pulled away Rafe realized Joshua had barely spoken. Was something up with his brother? He needed to make time to talk to him at the party, find out if anything was wrong. Because what affected one Boudreau, affected them all.

They were family.

CHAPTER TEN

Tessa's first view of the Big House stole her breath away. Several miles outside of Shiloh Springs, the sprawling acreage seemed to extend as far as she could see. Barbed wire fences lined the pasturelands, the land on both sides undulating outward in a sea of green. In the distance, she spotted cattle grazing. But as they rounded a gentle curve in the long driveway, she found she couldn't take her eyes off the house in the distance.

Huge by small town standards, heck by most people's standards, the homestead stretched outward, a two-story structure with an enormous wraparound porch. Tall magnolia trees stood as beacons, the two in the front providing shade and giving the place a feeling of permanence. Like it had always been there, and would be there for decades to come.

But most important was the sense of home she felt looking at the grand estate. It almost seemed to open its arms in welcome, beckoning her forward, whispering she belonged. It was a sensation, a feeling she'd never felt about a place before, and a tingling warmth spread through her the closer they got.

"It's amazing," she whispered.

"It is. The first time I saw this place, I was just a kid, but there was something about it. A sense once I stepped through those doors, my whole life would change. Best way I can describe the feeling…it felt like I was coming home." Rafe pulled onto the grass in front of the house, parking between two pickup trucks, one shiny and looking brand new, the other dented and rusty with the paint peeling and a weathered, sun-bleached appearance. Several more vehicles lined both sides of the front yard.

"I can't imagine growing up in a place like this. I'm pretty much a city girl. Cattle and horses, ranching, it's all new to me."

"The Boudreaus have lived here for several generations. This used to be one of the biggest spreads around, but Dad's heart wasn't in ranching. He went into the military, and when he came home, he worked in construction, building up his business from the ground up. All the Boudreaus since have worked for Boudreau Construction at some point, though only Liam still does. He handles the job sites, runs the crews. Dad deals with the business end of things, although he's been known to wield a hammer every now and again, to keep his hand in the game. We all pitch in from time to time if there's a need."

Rafe slid from the car and jogged around, opening her door before she could reach for the handle. A Southern girl through and through, raised in North Carolina, she occasionally had doors opened for her, but she still hadn't gotten used to the gallantry Texas men displayed, especially these Boudreau men. She had to admit, if only to herself, she liked it.

Opening the back door, he lifted out the cake box. Jill insisted Tessa take the cake with them, her gift to the Boudreaus, and asked her to express Jill's regret at not being able to come. The box contained one of her glorious baked creations. When she'd delivered it the night before, Tessa stared in awe, once again staggered by her friend's creativity and skill. Three tiers tall, somehow she'd managed to convey a sense of fireworks exploding, making the cake appear like an Independence Day extravaganza. The only thing missing was a band playing John Philip Sousa in the background. Though it wasn't July any longer, the cake was perfect for a Saturday afternoon barbecue at a place like the Boudreau spread. She wished Jill came with the cake, but she'd refused, stating she had something going on in Austin. Tessa didn't buy it, though. Something else kept her friend from partying with the rest of Shiloh Springs. If Jill didn't open up soon, she'd have to give her a none-too-gentle nudge. After all, she had experience dealing with Jill burying her emotions deep, and having to pry them out. She'd done it before, back when they'd been in school together.

The front door swung open, and a blonde whirlwind raced across the porch and launched herself at Rafe, skidding to a stop when she spotted the box in his hands. Grinning like the Cheshire cat who'd spotted a plump canary, she turned toward Tessa, and stuck out her hand.

"You're here! Hi, I'm Veronica Boudreau, but you can call me Nica. And you're Tessa. I've heard all about you from Momma. Come on, everybody's around back. Rafe, hurry up, you're already late."

"We're not late, squirt. We're right on time."

"Well, it feels like you're late. Besides, I couldn't wait to meet Tessa. I have the feeling we're going to be great friends." Wrapping her arm around Tessa's shoulder, she glanced toward her brother. "What's in the box?"

"Cake."

Nica stopped and spun around, taking Tessa with her, since she still had her arm around her shoulder. "*Cake?* You brought a cake? Rafe Boudreau, the man who can barely boil water, made a cake?"

Tessa wanted to giggle at the look of indignation on Rafe's face. Apparently his sister knew him well, and didn't mind giving him grief.

"Tessa brought the cake, I'm the pack mule." He shot a scorching glare at his sister, before mumbling under his breath, "I could have baked one if I wanted."

Nica patted her arm. "Good. You start training him right, right from the beginning. Makes 'em easier to handle in the long run." She leaned forward, peering through the box's cellophane lid, and turned to Tessa. "You made this?

It's gorgeous."

"No, my friend Jill made it. She's an amazing baker."

"Jill?" She turned toward Rafe, raising a brow. "Do I know this Jill?"

"Jillian Monroe, Dante Monroe's sister."

Nica nodded. "I remember her. She's sweet."

"Jill and I went to school together in North Carolina. That's where I first heard about Shiloh Springs."

"Can we move things along, ladies? This is getting heavy," Rafe nodded toward the cake, pretending to almost drop it. Tessa couldn't help noting the twinkle in his dark brown eyes as he teased his sister.

"Sorry, grouch. We're going." Nica winked at Tessa, and began tugging her once again toward the side of the house, Rafe trailing behind. Tessa tried to keep up with the younger woman, all the while taking in the beauty of the Boudreau home. The sound of voices and laughter wafted from the back of the house. Sounded like a lot of people, and for a second, nerves kicked in. When they rounded the corner, she spotted at least a couple dozen folks. A few of them she knew from sight—Liam, Lucas, and Brody—from her first days in Shiloh Springs. Others were parents of students she'd met, and a couple of the kids, some of whom who would soon be in her classroom.

"I know. They can be overwhelming. Keeping everybody straight is a challenge, but you'll get the hang of it pretty quick. Oh, look, Lucas is manning the grill with Dad. He's the best cook."

Glancing in the direction Nica pointed, Tessa spotted Lucas and Douglas Boudreau, standing beside a huge grill. It had to be at least ten feet long, built into the edge of the enormous patio at the back of the house. The patio itself was covered with a wooden pergola, the rustic beams decorated with glittering lights, which probably looked amazing at night. Chairs were scattered around the space, clustered into several groupings, making for intimate conversational areas. Off in the corner sat a fire pit. She could imagine the kids having a ball, making s'mores later in the afternoon, or roasting hotdogs after racing around and playing the day away.

"Tessa!" Ms. Patti called out, motioning her over toward a group of people seated on the outdoor furniture in a semicircular grouping, the petite woman holding court surrounded by her willing subjects. "I'd like you to meet the Fergusons. They're neighbors, and live on the other side of our property."

"It's a pleasure, Ms. Maxwell." A tall, silver-haired man stood, grasping her hand. Big and barrel-chested, he stood over six feet, broad across the shoulders with the beginnings of a paunch around his middle. He reminded her of a grizzly bear. Beside him, a plump, older woman smiled indulgently as he reached for her hand. "I'm William, and this is my beautiful bride, Beverly." Though she tried to hide her surprise at his unusual introduction, he must have read it, because he chuckled. "I always call her my bride, because I love her as much today as the day I married her, almost forty years ago."

It was one of those *aww* moments, and Tessa felt a warmth deep inside at the love shining in the man's eyes. *What would it be like, to have somebody love me like that?*

"Welcome to Shiloh Springs, Ms. Maxwell." Beverly Ferguson started to rise, but William's hand on her shoulder kept her seated, his touch gentle yet insistent.

"Honey, you need to stay off that ankle, remember?"

"How can I forget, Papa, when you remind me every time I stand up? The doctor said I could put a little weight on it."

"As long as it's still swollen, you're staying put." Though he said it with a smile, there was a core of solid steel behind his words. "Now, you ladies have a nice chat. I'm going over and see if the men need some help with the grill. Don't want to be serving burnt beef." He nodded, touched the brim of his hat, and sauntered off.

Beverly chuckled. "Darned old fool. Can't stand being cooped up with the womenfolk, but he hovers over me like a mama hen with her chicks. Barely lets me take a step without him holding me up. You'd think I broke both legs, instead of spraining my foot."

"Bev, he's worried. You did take a nasty fall." Ms. Patti scooted over on the love seat, making room for Tessa.

"A stupid, clumsy fall. Who ever heard of falling *up* the

stairs?"

Tessa shyly raised her hand. "My sister did once. She was volunteering at the hospital, working in the records room. They had a split-level space with four or five steps dividing the levels. She caught her foot on the bottom step, and fell up the stairs. She was wearing these strappy sandals, and ended up with bruising on her foot. It looked exactly like the shoe she had on. Couldn't walk on it for a few weeks."

Beverly chuckled. "Well, it helps to know somebody else did the same thing. Did mine climbing up the front porch steps. One minute everything was fine, the next—splat. I face-planted right into the shrubbery. Honestly, I'm more embarrassed than anything else."

Nica sat cross-legged on the ground beside her mother. Her long blonde hair flowed around her shoulders, and her soft brown eyes appeared almost golden in the sunlight. In the red-and-black plaid button-front shirt and jeans, she looked like she belonged, a part of the family and of the land surrounding them. Ms. Patti's hand absently smoothed along the top of her daughter's head, an almost reflexive movement, like it was something she did all the time.

"Momma, you should see the cake Tessa brought. I've never seen anything like it. It's stupendous!"

"Tessa, you didn't need to bring anything. We always have more food than we know what to do with," Ms. Patti protested. "I thank you, though, for your thoughtfulness." She tugged on a lock of Nica's hair. "Unlike some people."

"Not true, Momma. I think about helping—I just don't follow through." With an infectious grin, Nica shrugged, and Tessa laughed with everyone else. "Seriously, Momma, you should see the cake. Tessa said Jill Monroe made it."

"Jill? Why didn't she bring it herself? Isn't she coming?"

"She said she had business in Austin, but she sends her regrets." Tessa relayed Jill's message, beginning to wonder if there was something going on she wasn't seeing. Jill acted like she hadn't been invited, yet Ms. Patti's words made her think she'd been an expected guest.

Oh, yeah, Jill definitely has some explaining to do next time I see her. I think she's been holding out on me.

"I'll make sure and give her my thanks personally." From her tone, it sounded like Ms. Patti might be giving her more than thanks. More like a piece of her mind. The only thing missing from her sentence was *bless her heart*, which every Southern lady knows, if that's directed at you, you better run for the hills.

"Food's ready. Come and get it." At Douglas' yell, the squeal of excited kids overrode all talking. Tessa glanced around, taking in all the excited faces. The younger children raced past, headed for the tables, loaded with so much food she was surprised they didn't collapse beneath the weight. Expecting to see a lot of pushing and shoving, she was pleasantly surprised when the kids formed a line, paper plates in hand. Douglas spoke with each child, leaning forward to hear, before taking their plate and placing either a hamburger or hot dog on it, and handing it back.

"We feed the kids first. Once they've filled their little tummies, they'll head off to the play area, while the adults get a chance to actually sit down and enjoy their food." Ms. Patti watched the line move, her gaze straying constantly to her husband, and Tessa had no trouble reading the love in her expression.

"You ready to eat?"

The question came from behind her, and she craned her head around, finding Rafe there, his hand resting lightly on the back of the loveseat. He couldn't have been standing there long, or she'd have noticed him.

"Absolutely. I'm starving."

"Good, because Dad made enough to feed almost everybody in Shiloh Springs." Taking her arm, he led her to the table, and began piling two plates high with a little bit of everything.

"I can do it," she protested, but he simply smiled and kept piling on more food.

Finally, they walked over to the grill, where Douglas and Lucas stood waiting. A soft breeze blew, and the scent of the barbecued meat smelled amazing, making her mouth water. The ease with which the men handled the tongs and spatula showed they had plenty of experience with chefs' duty. Lucas' deep auburn hair blazed with fiery red highlights under the afternoon sun, since he'd tossed his hat aside earlier. Douglas' salt and pepper hair didn't show a hint of red, and Tessa wondered again why most of the boys looked nothing like either parent.

"What would you like, Tessa? We've got steak and ribs for the adults, or you can have a burger or hot dog if you prefer."

"Ribs, please. This is amazing, Mr. Boudreau."

He frowned and made a motion with the tongs in his hand. "What's this Mr. Boudreau nonsense? Told you to call me Douglas, or Doug if you prefer."

Heat flooded her cheeks. He had told her to call him by his Christian name, but somehow it didn't feel right. But, she'd do it if he insisted.

"Thank you, Douglas. Everything looks delicious."

He chuckled. "My Patti knows how to make folks happy. Feed 'em good and feed 'em a lot. Full bellies equals contented neighbors." When he started loading a full rack of ribs on her plate, she shook her head.

"Only half of that. I couldn't come close to finishing all those."

"Give her the whole rack, Dad. I'll help her eat them."

"Figured as much, son." Douglas added a huge burger to Rafe's plate, and turned back to the grill. "Come on back if you want more."

"Rafe," Lucas spoke for the first time since they'd been standing there. He been quietly studying them, and she really looked at him for the first time, wondering what he saw when he looked at her. Though he'd seemed a little quieter than the other Boudreaus, at least around her, this afternoon he seemed almost pensive. "Why don't you and Tessa go sit by the well? It'll be quieter over there. The kids

81

will be on the other side of the house playing. Give you a bit of privacy, and let you eat in peace."

If she hadn't been looking at Rafe, she'd probably have missed his start of surprise, an almost invisible question on his face. She glanced between the two brothers, wondering if there was some sort of silent communication going on, but when her stomach growled, she decided not to worry about it. The smells coming off the plate were enticing, and breakfast had been hours ago. She'd been too nervous about coming out to the Big House and mingling with all the Boudreaus to do more than nibble on a piece of toast with her coffee.

"Come with me, Tessa. I want to show you some-place...special."

Curiosity piqued, she followed him, carefully balancing her plate with one hand and her can of Dr Pepper with the other. He walked with the confident stride of a man who knew the land well. The kind of familiarity she associated with cowboys of the old west, his long-legged gait slow and deliberate. She had to admit, she found it kinda sexy.

They walked across the sprawling back deck teaming with adults and kids, chowing down on plates overflowing with barbecued meat and all the fixings that went along with it. Rafe nodded at the hellos from a few people, and Tessa smiled as she trailed in his wake. Soon they reached the edge of the patio and walked around the side of the house, where another small deck sat in front of a set of French doors. Several decorative urns and pots overflowing with deep green ferns and flowering plants were scattered over the concrete surface, their strikingly vivid colors evidenced somebody's green thumb. A comfortable-looking set of chairs and a glass table off to the side completed the charming vignette.

Continuing past, he walked through a stand of trees, maybe another twenty feet, before stopping. Her breath caught in the back of her throat, because the scene before her was...indescribable. Absolutely breathtaking. A white-roofed gazebo sat in the center of a clearing, surrounded by a stand of tall pine trees. Big enough to hold a dozen people comfortably, there was white lattice skirting around the bottom, and a circular roof perched over the top of the structure. It reminded her of something out of a fairy garden—and she was instantly entranced. Who expected something so ethereal in the middle of a working Texas ranch?

Intertwined around the base of the gazebo were climbing pink and white roses and tall ornamental grasses, lending to its otherworldly appearance, and she breathed in the heady perfume from the flowers.

Inside the gazebo, at the center of this enchanted structure, was something even more surprising. A well. The smooth stone and wooden structure should have looked incongruous in such a fantasy-styled setting, yet somehow it fit. A small wooden bucket attached by rope to a wooden arm with a handle, and her first thought was it reminded her of a wishing well.

With a smile, Rafe led her to a painted white bench

partially hidden away within the surrounding walls. Tiny Christmas lights ringed the tree bases, and all along the inside of the roof. Oh, what she'd give to see this magical spot at night! As if he read her mind, he flicked a switch, and smiled as the lights turned on, the soft golden glow causing her to gasp in wonder.

"This is…" She broke off, unable to think of the right words to describe the special spot.

"Momma's secret garden. She's worked on it for years, weeding and planting, until everything was exactly the way she pictured in her head. My dad cleared the spot for her years ago, and this is the end result."

"It's like something out of a fairy tale, only better."

"That's exactly the look she was aiming for. She'll be pleased you got her vision. Now dig in, before your ribs get cold."

So entranced by this magical hideaway, she'd forgotten about the plate of food in her hands, but his gentle reminder triggered her hunger, and she dug in. The potato salad was perfect, and the fruit refreshing. Biting into one of the heavily-sauced ribs, she couldn't hide her moan. The meat was cooked perfectly, falling off the bone tender, the sauce sweet and spicy and tangy, all at the same time.

Forgetting about ladylike manners, she dug in, giving a mock growl when Rafe reached for a rib. Grinning, she relented, handing over half the rack.

They ate in silence, and she groaned when she finished. Though there was still food on her plate, there was no way she could eat another bite. Rafe snagged her last rib, biting into it with gusto, and she wondered where he put it all. He'd finished everything on his plate, and some of hers to boot.

"I'm stuffed. Just roll me over, and I'll take a nap."

Taking her plate, he set them both on the ground beside the bench, along with the empty soda cans, and wrapped an arm around her shoulders. The move surprised her, but in a nice way. Leaning into him, she rested her head on his shoulder, and drew in a deep breath. "This is really nice."

"Yeah, it is."

They stayed that way for several minutes, and she allowed the peaceful silence to wash over her. Occasionally, the sound of children's laughter drifted toward them, but none were close enough to see. Finally lifting her head off his shoulder, she reached for his hand, threading her fingers with his.

"You promised to tell me why you and your brothers don't look like Ms. Patti and Douglas. I'm guessing you're adopted?"

Rafe brushed the hair from her cheek with his other hand, and a tingle of warmth sizzled along the skin where he touched. When he cupped her face gently, she stared intently into his eyes, willing him to kiss her.

"I'll tell you everything, Red. But first, there's something I've been dying to do since the moment I saw you."

"What?"

"This," he whispered, right before his lips touched hers.

CHAPTER ELEVEN

An instantaneous rush spread through him the second his lips touched hers. He savored the first taste of her, the woman who'd been haunting his thoughts and dreams from the moment he'd met her. His tongue swept across her lips, silently demanding she open to him, and dove deep when she complied without protest.

She tasted like heaven. It felt different than any kiss before. He could kiss her forever, until all the stars fell from the sky, and it still wouldn't be enough. Everything around them, the sounds of the others at the barbecue, the laughter of children playing, faded to nothing as he deepened the kiss. He couldn't hear anything except her soft sigh and the barely-there moan that escaped when she leaned into him.

She tilted her head ever-so-slightly, tangling her fingers in his hair, and he did the same, sliding his fingers into her glorious auburn hair, and tugged slightly to get her exactly where he wanted her. Finally, he pulled back, drew in a long breath, and stared into her beautiful blue eyes, reading the mix of surprise and barely-banked desire in their sapphire depths.

Pulling away from Tessa proved the hardest thing he'd ever done, but now wasn't the time or the place to take things further, no matter every molecule in his body screamed to keep going. Though the gazebo gave an illusion of solitude, they weren't alone. Not really. Most of his family and neighbors sat mere feet away, around the side of the house on the back patio. This secluded spot of paradise, Momma's gazebo with its wishing well, could be overrun with people at any second, and these moments with Tessa in his arms were private and special, not to be shared with anybody else.

Especially since he'd experienced the most earth-shattering kiss of his entire life. One he intended to repeat, as soon as they were someplace with a bit more privacy, and maybe four walls and a roof, away from any prying eyes.

She stared at him, her cheeks flushed a bright pink, and he couldn't resist brushing his thumb against the curve of her jaw. Felt the softness of her skin, like the dew-kissed petals of the gardenias beneath his bedroom window. Fragile and easily bruised, yet with gentleness and patience, they blossomed and flourished. Somehow, they reminded him of Tessa and her inner strength and resilience.

"Rafe?" Her voice was barely above a whisper, but he heard the tentative question at its heart. And he had promised her answers.

"I met Douglas Boudreau when I was eleven years old." Her eyes widened at his words, searching his face. The knot in the pit of his stomach expanded the second he'd uttered the words, and he suddenly wished he hadn't promised to tell her his story. Not because he was ashamed or didn't want her to know. No, because he didn't want to destroy the magic still racing through his veins from their kiss.

"You don't have to—"

He placed a finger against her lips, and continued as if she hadn't spoken. "It had been a particularly bad night. Though to tell you the truth, there weren't a lot of good days or nights when I was a kid. There hadn't been in a long time. My mother, my biological mother, was a wonderful woman. Sweet, kind, and funny. She made the mistake of falling in love with the wrong man." He ran a hand through his hair, searching for the right words. "My biological father wasn't a monster. Except when he was high. Things weren't bad at first, when I was little. By the time I turned nine, his habit tipped over into the out of control category."

"What did he take?" She voiced the question absently. He gritted his teeth, using every ounce of willpower to control his emotions. This was why he didn't talk about the past. The last thing he wanted or needed was to hear pity in her voice. Instead, he erected a wall, locking everything behind it, so nothing leaked out to destroy what he'd worked so hard to build—a new family and a new life. He wouldn't allow anybody to hurt him again—not even Tessa.

"Most days? Meth, but after a while, he'd use anything he could get his hands on. When he got high, he got violent.

Mom took the brunt of his anger, at least most of the time. Protected me and took the physical abuse herself. Of course, like most abusers, once he sobered up, he'd come home with an armload of flowers and gifts, swearing he'd never hit her again. We actually left twice. Moved into a shelter." He gave a bitter laugh, inwardly wincing at the ugly sound. "Gotta hand it to him. He somehow managed to talk her into coming back every time."

The rage he always felt when speaking about his biological father burned like acid in his veins. As a cop, he saw it all the time, especially when he'd worked in Dallas. Same story, different faces. He tried to distance himself, look at it dispassionately and objectively. Prayed he'd become a more compassionate man because he'd experienced what they did, but dealing with it as a cop and dealing with it as a victim— two entirely different realities.

"Things came to a head one stifling hot night in the middle of July. The temperatures had been in the hundreds for days. Mom finally reached the end of her rope. I'm not sure if was a combination of the weather and my dad's increasing drug use, but for whatever reason, she'd had enough. My father," he spat out the word, feeling it like a bitter taste on his tongue, "came home stoned again. Angry. Ready to take out his rage on the nearest target, which ended up being my mom. To this day, I don't remember what set him off. Could have been anything, because he had a hair trigger most days. Anyway, he threw a punch at her—and I stepped in."

"Rafe." Her hand squeezed his tight, the look on her face a combination of shock and compassion. But he didn't see the one emotion he'd dreaded. Pity. Too bad this wasn't the end of the story.

"I'd never been a big kid. Think scrawny with bones sticking out. I ended up flying across the kitchen. I smacked into the refrigerator, before landing on the linoleum. I definitely saw stars. That was the first time he hit me. I'm not talking about spankings and stuff. Trust me, I got plenty of those." Enough his teachers noticed the bruises and swelling on his arms and legs, but not enough to do a damned thing about it. There'd been more nights than he liked to remember where he'd been unable to sit down from the welts and open cuts caused by his old man's belt buckle across his backside and thighs. He'd learned to sleep on his stomach, to keep the blood off the sheets. He still carried scars, both physical and emotional.

"I don't need to hear any more."

Raising the hand still engulfed in his, he pressed a soft kiss against it, feeling its softness against his lips. "You need to understand what my life was like before, so you'll see why meeting Douglas Boudreau changed my whole world."

"I don't want you reliving it. Let the past stay in the past."

Unshed tears glistened in her eyes, sparkling like diamonds in the afternoon sunlight. Lifting his hand, he caught one on the tip of his finger, and his heart stuttered in his chest. Other than Ms. Patti, he couldn't remember the last time anyone had cried for him.

"Let me finish, sweetheart." He smiled and brushed a kiss against her cheek. "I promise it has a happy ending."

"Good. You deserve one."

He pulled her close against his side, and tucked her head onto his shoulder. Maybe if he didn't stare into her beautiful eyes, he'd get through it faster. Treat it like ripping off a Band-Aid. It hurt only for a moment before it faded.

He decided to skip the rest of what happened in the kitchen of that rundown trailer, with the hole in the bathroom floor big enough to see the rocks and weeds beneath, and the missing windows in the one bedroom, covered over by cardboard boxes his mother had stolen from the back of a liquor store and held in place with duct tape. Not that it was any different from the succession of mobile homes and bug-infested, rent-by-the-hour motel rooms which dotted his childhood.

"My old man finally passed out in front of the TV, but not before polishing off half a case of beer. Mom…bled from her nose and mouth, where he'd punched her in the face. Only this time, I could tell she'd had enough. Don't know if it was because he'd hit me, or if she'd simply reached the end of her rope, but she was done. Done with all of it. Him. The crappy motel rooms and broken down, rusted out cars, the never enough money for food, but whatever the cause, it was the last straw. Anyway, terrified she'd wake him if we went out the front door, we snuck out." He didn't tell her how he'd kicked out the cardboard-covered bedroom window, and made his mom go first, just in case. Tessa didn't need to hear all the gory details, the ones that haunted him still in his nightmares when he let his guard down. "We made it to the end of the drive before he stumbled out of the house, carrying a baseball bat."

"Oh, my—"

He continued as if she hadn't spoken, because he needed to get through this. "Mom drove like a bat out of hades. I kept watch out the back window, scared he'd catch up." *Scared? More like terrified I'd crap my pants if the monster caught up, because this time I knew he'd kill us both.* "We didn't live in Shiloh Springs. We'd been staying one town over. I think my mom headed this way deliberately, knowing he wouldn't dare step foot in this town. He'd had one too many run-ins with the county sheriff and outstayed his welcome. I always guessed that's why she headed in this direction." His laugh sounded brittle and ugly, reflective of the emotions roiling in the pit of his stomach. It wasn't often he voluntarily relived that night, but if he meant to have any chance of starting something between him and Tessa, she needed to know the truth—the good, the bad, and the ugly.

"He drove this piece of sh—junk truck. I'm not sure how he kept it running, because it had to be held together with rubber-bands and duct tape. Not that Mom's car was much better. Between the bad starter and bald tires, there's no way it would have passed state inspection." He shook his head, trying to dislodge the memory of what happened next, not wanting the picture too fresh in his mind. Though it had happened two decades ago, the memory remained sharp and crisp. The sound of metal-on-metal when his dad's truck slammed into the rear passenger side of the car. The screech of tires, struggling to grip the asphalt with their threadbare treads. The acrid stench of smoke and gasoline when the front end plowed into the live oak tree on the side of the road. The jolt of impact. Seeing the crumpling of the front end of the car where it collided with the tree, the shattered windshield crisscrossed with spiderweb cracks.

"I was sitting in the back seat when he hit us." Her sharp gasp made him pause, and squeeze her hand tight. "The car went engine first into a tree. I got thrown onto the floorboards, and hit my head against the seat. The airbags worked, because I remember powder floating all around me. My father broke the driver's window when he couldn't get the door open, and pulled my mom out of the car. Stupid me—I thought he meant to help her."

"Did he come back for you?"

Rafe shook his head. "I don't think he even remembered I was there. He tossed my mom to the ground like she was nothing. A pile of trash. Baby, the rage on his face—"

"I get the picture. He didn't deserve you, either of you."

"He hit her. Punched her in the face repeatedly. When

she tried to crawl away, he kicked her over and over. I remember screaming at the top of my lungs, but nothing came out. Wrenching at the door, but it wouldn't budge. The car hit the tree with such force, the frame bent. I threw myself against the door, pounded on it, but it didn't move, wouldn't open. It never occurred to me to climb out the window he'd busted to pull her out on the driver's side. To him, I wasn't even there. Every ounce of his attention seemed focused on my mother. I heard sirens, saw the flashing lights, but my brain couldn't comprehend help was on the way."

"Douglas?"

Brushing his thumb gently across her cheek, he smiled. "Yeah. The sheriff's car pulled up along with the fire department rescue squad. They physically restrained my father, had to pull him off because he wouldn't stop beating my mom." He took a deep breath. "I knew before they said anything they were too late. She was gone."

"I'm so sorry, Rafe."

"It didn't seem real, you know? I could see everything. Hear people talking, moving around, but it didn't sink in. Nothing did. I know they used the Jaws of Life to get me out, because they couldn't budge the door, either. But the only thing I could see was this giant of a man, standing by the car, working with the rest of them to free me. Why him and not one of the other men working frantically, I don't know, yet I knew I could trust him to keep me safe."

Though they sat in the midst of his mother's special garden, the gazebo and wishing well disappeared. The sounds of kids playing faded away under a barrage of memories from the night everything changed. He'd lost a part of himself, watching the monster who'd spawned him murder his mother. Felt a yawning blackness threatening to engulf his very soul. Until he met the kind gaze of a stranger. One he instinctively knew held his future, his salvation, within his hands.

"They got me out, put me on a gurney, and I reached out to the man standing there. I didn't know him. Had no clue who this man was, other than he was my lifeline. I think I begged him to stay with me, though I don't remember. The way Ms. Patti tells it, I grabbed his hand and wouldn't let go." He chuckled. "Anyway, he rode with me to the hospital. Waited in the emergency room, and talked with the doctors. A time or two he ordered people around, making sure I got taken care of. A whole lot of that night is kinda sketchy. I was pretty much out of it. When I woke the next morning, he was still there. Sitting beside my bed. He told me I was coming home with him." He had to stop, the words catching in his throat.

"I think I'm a little in love with Douglas now. I'm sorry about your mom."

Pulling her closer against his side, he nuzzled his chin against the top of her head. "Thank you. She did the best she could, and I will always love her for it."

"Can I ask…what happened to your father?"

He paused a moment before answering. "He's in Huntsville for second-degree murder. Serving a life sentence without the possibility of parole."

"Not to sound bloodthirsty, but good."

His body shook with suppressed laughter. "You sound like Ms. Patti. If she'd had her way, he'd be buried under the jail."

"In case you haven't learned this, Sheriff, women can be a bit vengeful. Especially if somebody goes after a person we…care about."

He drew in a deep breath, feeling an enormous weight lift from his shoulders. While he'd left out a lot of the gory details, Tessa now knew his history, and she didn't seem repulsed his biological kin was rotting in a Texas prison for murder. Though it didn't happen often, a few smallminded folks tarred him with the same brush as his father, simply because of the blood coursing through his veins. Nature versus nurture didn't mean a whole lot to some people.

"Now you know how I came to be a Boudreau. All of us have our own story. Douglas and Ms. Patti opened their home, and their hearts, to a whole bunch of misfits and troublemakers nobody else wanted, and molded us into a family."

"They are very lucky to have you too."

He brushed a light kiss across her forehead before standing. "I'm the lucky one, babe. I'm blessed with a home and a family who, while they might not be blood, are *more* because we chose to become one. There isn't anything I wouldn't do for every single one of my brothers and sister, and I know they feel the same."

"I like that—blessed."

He picked up their empty plates and soda cans. "We should probably get back to the party before somebody comes looking for us."

He stopped when he felt her hand lightly touch his forearm. "Thank you for sharing today with me, Rafe."

"My pleasure, sweetheart."

As they headed back to join his family, he couldn't help feeling today marked a turning point in his relationship with Tessa. He really cared for her, more than he had for anybody in a long time, and couldn't help wondering what the future held, and honestly, he couldn't wait to find out.

CHAPTER TWELVE

Rafe pulled up in the driveway of her house, and left the engine running. Climbing out, he opened her door and walked her to the front porch. Her mind still reeled from everything he'd told her at the barbecue. About his childhood. His life with the Boudreaus. The next time she saw Douglas Boudreau, she planned on giving him a gigantic hug.

She started to ask if he wanted to come in for coffee, but he pressed a finger against her lips, before leaning forward and kissing her cheek.

"I can't stay. I'm on duty in a few hours, and need to get some sleep before I head in." He gave a roguish grin before adding, "Besides, if I come inside, I'm not sure I'd be strong enough to leave again, and it's too soon. I don't want to make a mistake or spoil things before they've even started."

A tiny bit of her felt disappointed, even if he was right. "Thanks for inviting me to your family's cookout, Rafe. I had a lovely time. And you're right, it's too soon." She didn't mention the things they'd discussed, the feelings too new and raw. Though she knew she'd think about them, a lot.

"Dinner? Tomorrow night?"

She studied his face intently before nodding. "I'd like that."

"I'll call you in the morning, and we'll set something up." He reached for her hand, and brushed a soft kiss against her knuckles. "Goodnight, Red."

"'Night, Sheriff."

Climbing the front steps, she unlocked the door and waved, watching as he pulled out and drove toward his house. Turning to go inside, she spotted four boxes stacked neatly by the porch swing. Darn it, she'd forgotten the courier had been scheduled to drop them off today. They must have delivered them while she'd been at the Boudreau house. Tossing her purse onto the hall table, she toted each box inside, setting them down in the living room.

Carefully labeled in her sister's precise handwriting, she ran her hand along the label, tracing the name of her old home town. An ache in the center of her chest squeezed tighter as she realized the things contained within these boxes held her last physical ties to North Carolina, other than Beth and Jamie. Specifically, they were things belonging to her parents, items too personal or sentimental to get rid of or donate. She'd gone back to her parents' home with Beth, shortly after they'd passed, and cleared out the house, each keeping the things holding value to them, and the rest sold or donated to charitable causes.

She remembered the ache of loneliness deep inside at the

realization their house would no longer be her home. The place where she'd spent endless hours playing or listening to music. Remembered the back bedroom, with its pretty floral bedspread—the one she'd picked out herself when she'd turned thirteen—thinking how grown up and mature she'd felt, decorating her room. Beth and Evan had their own home, one they'd bought right after they married, much bigger and grander than the small home her parents owned. Yet, Tessa knew she wouldn't be able to live in that house alone. Not with all the memories of her parents, and knowing they'd taken their last breaths there.

The decision to sell had been mutual, but hadn't made it any easier. So, she'd kept the things which meant something, and now all that remained of her life in North Carolina sat contained in these four cardboard boxes. It seemed so insignificant, and couldn't compare to the scope of wonderful memories she'd shared with her family. Her fingers itched to pick up the phone and call Beth.

Nostalgia swept through her, and before she gave in to the urge to wallow in melancholy, she picked up the scissors, cutting through the packing tape on the first box. Before she'd left, driving straight through to Shiloh Springs, she'd carefully wrapped each cherished item. Placed them into the boxes herself, making sure there was more than enough bubble wrap and newspaper to protect the contents.

She gasped when she peeled back the flaps of the box, looking at the chaos inside. Something was wrong. The bubble wrap was shoved aside, wadded up in clumps, and half the items lay unprotected. Could this have happened in transit? Sometimes courier services weren't exactly gentle, even when the package stated fragile in big, bold letters.

Digging inside, she found a ceramic bowl on top which previously had been on the bottom. She remembered, because she'd been extremely careful, wrapping it with extra wrap, because her mother loved it so. Holding it to her chest, she looked deeper in the box. Nothing looked the way it had when she'd taped it shut a few weeks ago. What in the world happened?

Setting the blue and white bowl on the coffee table, she went to work on the tape of the second box. Maybe it was only the one box. Except the contents of this one looked the same as the first—nothing like the way she'd packed them. Attacking the third box, she found the same thing. And the fourth—everything inside was topsy-turvy.

Frantic now, she dug through each item, desperate to see if anything was missing or damaged. After lifting free the wooden box that had belonged to her father, she stood back and stared. Nothing appeared missing. Could she be wrong? In her rush to get everything packaged and ready to send to Texas, had she been mistaken?

Nope, she remembered how she'd packed. Beth even teased her about being a little OCD with the overwrapping. Picking up her phone, she dialed her sister's number. Beth would know what happened. The phone rang and rang, before finally a male voice answered.

"Hello?"

"Evan, it's Tessa."

"Tessa! How's everything in the Lone Star State? Are you getting settled in?"

"Things are great. I love it here. Can I talk to Beth?"

"She's in bed. Jamie's got a bit of a cold, and hasn't been sleeping well, so Beth was up with her most of last night. They went to bed early."

Tessa looked at the time on her phone and winced. She'd forgotten about the hour time difference between them. "Sorry, I didn't realize...could you have her give me a call in the morning?"

There was a slight pause, before Evan asked, "Is something wrong? You sound a little, I don't know, agitated."

Tessa blew out a long breath. "I got the boxes she shipped. Something's wrong with them. Everything is messed up, and—"

"That's my fault," he interrupted, leaving Tessa dumbfounded. "Beth went to her yoga class, and I was supposed to watch Jamie. I took a call from the office, and by the time I came back in the room, she'd pulled all the packing tape off the boxes, and had half the contents spread across the floor. I rewrapped everything the best I could, but I guess I didn't do a very good job. Is anything broken? I'll pay to get it fixed."

"Everything's fine. Nothing's missing or broken. Things were just...not the way I'd packed them. But I can't blame

102

Jamie for being curious. She's at that age. Thanks for repacking my stuff."

"No problem." There was another pause, before Evan whispered, "Could you maybe not tell Beth? I don't want her to find out I let Jamie out of my sight for more than a second when she wasn't here."

"My lips are sealed. Tell Beth I'll give her a call in a couple of days. Good night, Evan."

"Goodbye, Tessa."

Hanging up, she began gathering all the packaging scattered around the living room and tossed it all into one box, deciding everything could wait for tomorrow. The Boudreaus invited her to attend church with them in the morning, and she wanted to get a good night's sleep.

Tomorrow she'd add her parents' things to the house, find the perfect place for each one. Maybe putting her family's cherished belongings around the cottage would make it feel more like home, because she really liked Shiloh Springs, and could see making the town her home for longer than the year she'd initially planned. She wouldn't mind making this change permanent.

CHAPTER THIRTEEN

Tessa stared at the ringing phone, the queasy feeling in the pit of her stomach growing stronger. She didn't get a lot of calls. But for the last three days, whenever she'd answered, there hadn't been anybody on the other end.

Her hand shook when she swiped to connect and put the phone to her ear.

"Hello?"

Dead air. Yet she knew somebody waited on the other end, because she could hear them breathing. Not the creepy, obscene, trying-to-freak-you-out-type, but as if somebody simply listened, without saying a word.

"Look, I don't know who this is, but if you don't stop calling, I'm going to report you to the phone company and the sheriff's department. Stop harassing me!"

Hitting the end call button made her feel better, at least for a few seconds. Until it rang again. The incessant jangle of the bell pealed through the house's empty silence. Looking at the caller ID, it showed caller unknown. With a few simple keystrokes, she'd blocked the number.

"Nope, not falling for it again. Go bug somebody else."

Great, now they've got me talking to myself.

She balled her hands into fists to keep from reaching for the cell phone. A ringing phone always made her want to immediately pick it up, and she bit back the urge to respond. Finally, after what seemed an eternity, the ringing stopped, and she exhaled a long breath.

Seconds later, it rang again, and she nearly jumped out of her skin, chiding herself for being skittish. She glared at the phone, lying on the coffee table. Steeling herself, she lifted it and looked at the caller ID. Rafe's name and number displayed, and she collapsed against the sofa cushions, relief coursing through her.

"Hi."

"Tessa?" After a slight pause, barely longer than a heartbeat, "What's wrong?"

"Nothing." *Liar.*

"Red, do I need to come over?" His words were laced with concern, overshadowing her feeling of dread, and made her realize she'd probably overexaggerated the menace behind the stupid calls.

"Sorry. No, it's fine. My foolish imagination got away from me for a second."

"Something scared you?"

"Honestly, Rafe, it's probably nothing." She reached up and twined her finger in her hair, curling the ends round and round, a nervous habit she thought she'd broken. Should she tell him? Granted, the caller ID showed the caller was unknown, and it might be kids making crank calls, but…

"Tell me anyway." His tone brooked no argument, and she had no trouble picturing the scowl he most likely sported. A combination of I'm-not-taking-any-nonsense-from-you and I-only-want-to-help. It was a sign of his strength and caring, and what made him a good sheriff.

"Okay, but it's really nothing. The last couple of days, I've been getting calls. Whenever I pick up, nobody's there."

"How often is it happening?"

"One call on the first day, and a couple the next. Today, I threatened to report them to the phone company and the sheriff's department and hung up. The phone rang again almost immediately, but I didn't pick up. Afterward, I blocked the number."

Right then, the phone vibrated in her hand, startling her into almost dropping it.

"Check the caller ID, read it to me." His deep voice brooked no refusal.

Of course, it was the same ID of unknown caller, with a different number listed. Shoot, if it was teens playing a prank, they were pretty smart to use more than one phone to harass her.

"It's the same as before, unknown, but it's a different number," she told him.

"I'm on my way."

"Rafe, you don't have to—"

"Red, let me do my job. I'll be there in five minutes, ten

at the most."

"Thanks."

Though she hated to admit it, a small part of her rejoiced Rafe insisted on coming. With the calls becoming more frequent, her already skittish nerves were getting a workout. Coupled with the fact for the last couple of days she'd felt like somebody watched her every move, and she found herself jumping at any little noise.

Before five minutes had elapsed, Rafe pulled into her drive and parked behind her car. His long-legged gait ate up the distance to the door, and she pulled it open before he'd made it to the porch.

She didn't stop to think, barreling straight into his arms. They wrapped around her like bands of steel, shielding her from the world, and she leaned her head against his shoulder. If only she could get her body to stop shaking, everything would be alright.

"Shh, sugar, I'm here." A hand stroked down her spine, a soothing caress, and she leaned closer, inhaling his spicy scent. Standing in his arms, in the middle of her front porch where everyone could see them, a feeling of rightness swept through her, along with a feeling she'd finally come home.

With a reluctance she didn't fully understand, she pulled back, stepping out of his arms. "Sorry about that. I'm not usually such a watering pot." Turning, she led him into the house.

"I didn't mind. You can use my shoulder anytime." The

gentleness in his voice matched the sweetness of his smile, making her eyes tear up again. She sat on the edge of the sofa, her hands in her lap, clenched tightly together. Darn it, she needed to stop shaking.

"Tell me about the calls. You said they started a couple of days ago?"

She gave a quick nod. "The first time it happened, I figured it was a wrong number. That happens all the time with cellphones."

"Yes, it does. But the calls kept happening—like today?"

"Today has been the worst. Every time it rings, I'm afraid to pick it up and see unknown caller on the screen." She forced a laugh, trying to make light of the situation. "I'm probably blowing everything out of proportion. It could be kids getting their jollies, or even robo-calls that hang up when they connect to another number."

"The way you're shaking tells me you don't really believe it, Tessa. What aren't you telling me?"

Running her hand through her hair, she raised her gaze to his. "It may be nothing, but before I moved here, I'd had a little trouble with an ex-boyfriend." She watched the way his eyes flashed, saw the tightening in his hands.

"Define a little trouble."

"Not long after my parents died, Trevor's actions began changing. He started getting a little more…I guess you'd call it demanding. Almost possessive. Wanting to always know where I was. Who I was with. He started showing up without notice at my job. Or at the restaurant, when I went to lunch with Beth. I have to admit, at first, it didn't seem like a big deal. It was flattering to be the center of attention."

She saw the moment he understood. He was a good cop, and easily read between the lines. "We're talking a jealous ex."

"Yeah. He didn't want me seeing any of my friends. He'd make plans for us, yet didn't include people I knew, and he'd get mad if I even wanted to spend an evening with my sister. At first, I admit I ate up the attention because I'd been devastated by my parents' deaths, functioning on autopilot most of the time, and Trevor helped me pick up the pieces."

"You mean he took advantage of you when you were at your lowest point."

She hated how weak and pathetic that made her sound, even if it was the truth. She shrugged. "About four months ago, I worked up the nerve to break things off. I thought it was a clean break. He seemed to take the news well. He even left me alone for a few weeks. Then he'd show up at my place. Or call. Text. Act like we were still a couple, like nothing had changed. Even my brother-in-law, Evan, talked to him, told him to back off. Nothing worked."

"Did you contact the police? Get a restraining order against him?"

She bit the inside of her cheek to keep from saying something she'd regret. "I may be foolish, Rafe, but I'm not stupid. When he didn't give up, I went to the police. They sent an officer to talk to Trevor, and told him he needed to stay away. Once the police talked to him, he finally got the message and stopped calling and coming around. That's why I don't think he's doing this."

"Did you change your number when you moved to Shiloh Springs?"

"No, it's the same."

He reached across the space dividing them, and clasped both her hands within his. "I'm going to look into this, see what I can find out. I'll add your ex to the list—" He broke off when she shook her head vehemently. "Tessa, I wouldn't be doing my due diligence if I didn't investigate all possibilities, and that includes your former boyfriend."

"Honestly, I think Trevor has moved on, but do what you have to." She gave him a tentative smile. "You're the sheriff."

"And don't you forget it." At his exaggerated wink, she giggled.

Giggling? What am I, twelve?

"You okay now, sweetheart? I can stay if you need me."

"Thanks, Rafe. I'm probably blowing this all out of proportion. Maybe it's somebody dialing the wrong number, and I'm making too big a deal out of it."

"I'm gonna check it out anyway." He slipped on his cowboy hat, the brim shadowing his face. She'd never thought she'd fall for the kind of man who spoke with a slow drawl, wore a Stetson and boots, but she admitted, if only to herself, this particular cowboy made her heartbeat go pitter-pat.

Impulsively, she wrapped her arms around his shoulders, hugging him, and his arms slid around her, pulling her close. Again, she breathed in deep, branding his scent into her memory.

"Lock your doors to be on the safe side until we figure this out. I'll let you know as soon as I hear anything."

"Thanks again, Rafe."

With a final look over his shoulder, he was gone, and she closed the door, sliding the bolt home. Leaning her back against the cool wood, she sighed before heading to the bedroom office.

She hoped he found out something soon, because she refused to live her life in fear.

Rafe leaned back in his office chair, and propped his booted feet onto the desk, holding the phone to his ear. Acid burned in his gut as he considered the eerie phone calls Tessa had gotten. Maybe it was kids playing a practical joke on the new teacher, but he wasn't taking any chances.

"Hey bro, got a favor to ask."

"What, no hello, how've you been? Straight to asking for something." His brother, Antonio, chuckled. "Good to hear from you too, Rafe. What's up?"

"Need to know if you've got an expert who can trace incoming calls to a cell phone. The number shows up as unknown caller. Once it's blocked, the caller uses a different number. Is there any way to determine who's making the calls, or where they're coming from?"

The first person he'd thought to call with Tessa's problem? His brother, Antonio, who worked with the FBI office in Dallas. He had sources Rafe didn't have in the much smaller Shiloh Springs. And Rafe didn't mind exploiting his brother's connections if it meant protecting Tessa.

"What's going on?"

"Someone's been making harassing calls to Tessa, and I'm trying to figure out where they're coming from. She can tell somebody's on the other end because she hears them breathing."

"Tessa? You mean the new teacher?"

"Yeah. She moved here from North Carolina, and doesn't have a clue who would be calling her from an unknown number. She's got in her head it's probably kids playing pranks, but I'm not so sure." He could almost hear the wheels spinning in Antonio's head at his answers, and knew his brother probably had a million questions of his own.

"Give me the cell number that's receiving the calls, and I'll have a buddy look into it. Not sure how much information he can get, unless we put a tracker on her phone. But will do what we can." There was a long pause, before Antonio spoke again. "Could this be somebody from her past…maybe somebody from North Carolina?"

Rafe didn't want to consider there might be somebody back in North Carolina from Tessa's past who'd want to hurt her—or worse. But it was a distinct possibility, especially after their conversation earlier. Somebody she'd cared about—or even loved. But Rafe was a cop. He couldn't afford to look at this from a personal aspect, even if it made his head ache. It also meant he'd have to do a little digging into Tessa's past.

"How much information do you think you can obtain from cell phone calls showing an unknown caller?"

"Depends. There are a lot of factors to figuring out where a call came from, whether a landline or cell phone, trying to track the towers and where the call generated, but…"

"But it's a long shot, right?"

Antonio sighed. "Yeah, you haven't given me a lot to go on here, and it's going to be almost impossible to trace, but we'll give it our best shot. I know a guy who's one of the best at cell phone data, locating the towers where a call pinged, and maybe we'll get lucky."

Rafe ran a hand through his hair, frustration eating at him. There had to be more he could do. He hadn't made any promises to Tessa, but he knew worry would eat at her. As much as she tried to hide it, she didn't have a poker face, and her fear had coated his skin, thick and pungent.

"I appreciate it, bro."

"This Tessa, she's special?"

"I don't know, Antonio, there's something about her that calls to me in a way I've never felt before. I'm not sure I can put into words exactly why I'm so drawn to her, but there it is."

"Wish I could have been at the Big House when you brought her over. I know Momma raved about her the last time I called. I get the feeling she'd approve if you're thinking about getting serious."

"One thing at a time, bro. First, let's find out who's harassing Tessa and why."

Antonio's chuckle rang in his ears, and Rafe's shoulders relaxed. Not that it mattered, but he knew his brother would like Tessa. Heck, the whole family had welcomed her with open arms from the moment she'd landed in Shiloh Springs. He couldn't blame them; he'd been fascinated too.

"I'll call you as soon as I know anything. You find out anything else on your end, shoot me a text."

"Will do. Thanks."

"No problem."

After hanging up, Rafe headed for the door. Time to do his last drive through town, make sure things were quiet for the night. A habit ingrained from his predecessor, he took a half hour or forty-five minutes at the end of his shift, meandering through the back streets of Shiloh Springs.

Sometimes he found trouble and stopped it before it took hold. Other times, trouble found him.

And on the way home, he'd mosey past Tessa's house, and take a quick look around.

Nothing stirred his cop's instincts while he patrolled, so he radioed dispatch and signed off for the night. Within minutes, he parked across the street from Tessa's place, and turned off the engine. Pulling his hat low across his eyes, he hunkered down in his seat.

He'd gone without sleep before—what was one more night?

CHAPTER FOURTEEN

The next two weeks passed faster than he could blink. Sitting behind his desk at the sheriff's department, Rafe worked on the endless reams of paperwork which never seemed to grow smaller. This was the part of the job he disliked. He wouldn't call it hate, but it came awfully close. Give him a bad guy to chase down, or corralling a drunk to sleep it off, great. Paperwork? He shuddered.

Being the sheriff of a county the size of Shiloh Springs wasn't the same as working in the big city, which he'd done for a few years, once he'd graduated from Texas A&M. He'd contemplated going into the Army, intent of becoming a Green Beret, but when a fellow classmate joined the Dallas Police Academy, he convinced Rafe there was a better way he could serve his country closer to home. He'd graduated with honors at the top of his class, and never regretted the decision to become a cop.

The only problem was living and working in the big city wasn't all it was cracked up to be. More and more, he'd found himself thinking about Douglas and Ms. Patti, and Shiloh Springs. It might be cliché to say home is where the heart is, but it didn't make it any less true. Moving back and joining the sheriff's department as a deputy sheriff felt like sliding into a comfortable pair of boots. Two years later, he'd advanced to lead deputy sheriff, and when Sheriff Lassiter retired, he'd been named the new chief.

Glancing up, he spotted Dusty Sinclair leaning on the doorjamb, a piece of paper in his hand. "Boss, Jeb Grady called again. Looks like, and I quote, 'hooligans done trespassed onto my property again, and spray painted graffiti stuff all over the side of the henhouse, and you'd better damned well get off your lazy backside and get over here double quick'."

Rafe scrubbed a hand through his hair, giving a weary sigh. Why couldn't the boys from the high school pick another target, and leave Grady alone? Seemed like at least once a month, he'd get called out to handle some foolishness. Last month, some kids took potshots at his barn. The month before, they'd knocked down his mailbox. Would it ever end?

"Have dispatch give him a call, tell him I'll be out there this afternoon."

"Want me to take it? You've had your hands full..."

"Appreciate the offer, Dusty, but I've got it. I'm headed out anyway, so I'll swing by Grady's place."

"If you're sure," Dusty crossed his arms, his posture relaxed, though his expression was anything but. "Boss, I don't want to overstep my bounds, but I'm gonna say this anyway. You have got to learn to delegate. You work too hard as it is. We all see it. Let me or one of the others deal with this."

Rafe studied the tall man, who'd been working there for almost two years. Dusty Sinclair had moved to Shiloh Springs, relocating from Houston, wanting to be part of smaller town life and a slower pace. Maybe Dusty was right, and he'd been too blind to see it.

"You're right. But, since I'm already heading out, I'll handle Grady this time. Why don't you check with Brody over at the fire station? See if they're any closer to figuring out how the fire started last week."

Dusty straightened and gave him a mock salute. "I'm on it. If there aren't any important calls, why don't you take the rest of the afternoon off? You've earned it."

Standing, Rafe stretched, feeling the stiff muscles in his back protest the movement. He'd sat too long, dealing with the paperwork. Glancing at his watch, he smiled. If he hurried, maybe he could take Tessa to lunch before he headed south of town.

"Good idea, Dusty. I think I'll do that. Call me if anything needs my attention, otherwise, once I've dealt with Grady's problem, I'm done for the day. I'll let dispatch know on my way out."

Dusty grinned and walked away. Rafe slapped on his hat, and followed behind him, stopping beside the dispatcher's desk to let her know about the change in plans. Shiloh

Springs wasn't a tiny town, but they were small enough one dispatcher per shift normally handled the incoming calls, as well as notifying the officers on duty when a situation arose.

Within minutes, he'd driven to the elementary school, and spotted Tessa's car in the faculty parking lot, along with a couple others he recognized. He saw Tessa exiting the school, arms loaded with a cardboard box overflowing with papers. Grinning, he sprinted toward her, quickly closing the distance between them.

"Here, let me help you." Against her protest, he took the box from her hands.

"Rafe, what are you doing here?" He nearly chuckled at the surprise on her face. It had been several days since he'd seen her, though he'd called to check and make sure she was doing okay. That's what neighbors did, right?

"Thought I'd drop by, see if I could take our newest teacher to lunch."

"Lunch? Is it that late already?"

"Yep. I have one quick stop, then I thought we might head over to Juanita's Café for some Tex-Mex. Sound good?" Opening his car's rear door, he slid the box onto the back seat and straightened, waiting for her answer.

"If you're sure it isn't a bother. I love Tex-Mex." At her grin, he felt a tingling sensation in the center of his chest, spreading warmth through him. What was it about this woman that made him alternately feel ten feet tall and like a thirteen-year-old with his first crush? Whatever it was, he wanted to explore it, find out what made Tessa Maxwell different than anybody he'd ever met.

"Perfect." He held open the passenger door, and she slid onto the seat. Within seconds, he was headed south. Dealing with Jeb Grady shouldn't take long, and then he'd get to spend some quality time with Red.

He drove for a few miles before she asked, "Where are we heading?"

"Jeb Grady called in a complaint some kids spray painted graffiti all over the side of his henhouse. Give me a few minutes to take a look, get some pictures, and we'll be on our way."

"Wow, I thought graffiti was more of an inner city thing. Didn't expect to run into crime in small town Texas."

He shook his head, glancing her way for a moment before turning back to watch the road. "Shiloh Springs is no different than any other city, big or small. Crime is crime, and people break the law everywhere."

"Living in a large city like Charlotte, I guess you become inured to the crime around you. Especially when it doesn't personally touch your life. The closest I've ever come was when the police came to investigate my parents' deaths."

He straightened a little in his seat. This was the first time she'd mentioned an investigation concerning her parents. He knew they'd passed away, remembered his mother telling him something about it, but Tessa hadn't voluntarily broached the subject before now. Couldn't hurt to probe a little, find out a bit more about the woman who'd become his secret fascination.

"Why'd the police investigate? I'm not trying to pry." *Oh, yes, I am.* "You haven't talked much about your folks."

She swiveled to face him, as much as the seatbelt would allow. "I didn't realize. I guess I don't talk about them because it still hurts. They've only been gone for several months. Some days it seems like they've been gone forever, yet others, it seems like it happened yesterday." Her hands tugged at the hem of her blouse, and he fought the urge to reach out and grasp them, to offer his silent comfort.

"Tell me about them. They must have been extraordinary to have raised a woman like you."

He watched a blush wash across her cheeks, the pink bringing a glow to her face. Didn't she realize how different she was from other women? Maybe not, but he saw it, and knew others did too. His family adored her, inviting her to sit with them at church on the family pew. Especially his momma, who invited her to visit again this coming Sunday, and that invitation included dinner at the Big House.

"Daddy was an amazing man." Tessa stared out the windshield as she spoke, a wistful look on her face. "Larger than life, with more love in his heart than ten men. He was a teacher too. He taught political science at the community college near their house. Mom was a stay-at-home mother when Beth and I were younger. After we reached middle school, she got a part-time job as a receptionist at a doctor's office. Always made sure she was there every day when we got home from school."

"Sounds like you had great parents."

He couldn't help thinking about how different her childhood had been from his—which hadn't been ideal— until he'd been lucky enough to become a part of the Boudreau family. Though he'd shared the bare bones of his story the day he'd taken her to the barbecue at the Big House, she didn't know all the details of what his life was like before. And now wasn't the time or the place for conversation. It would happen later—if at all.

"They were the best. One of the hardest things I ever did was move away my junior year of college. Until then, I lived at home and commuted back and forth. They didn't mind me sticking around. In fact, they encouraged it because it meant more time together. We weren't rich," she chuckled, "not on a college teacher's salary, but Beth and I never went without."

She absently brushed at a tear, and he fought the urge to pull over to the side of the road and pull her into his arms. Comfort her. Ease the ache she obviously felt. But there wasn't a thing he could do. He couldn't tell her everything would be okay; it wasn't a promise he could make. Nobody knew what tomorrow held. But he'd be damned if he wouldn't try to make her life better any way he could.

"You miss them."

"Every single day."

"What happened?"

"Carbon monoxide poisoning. They died in their sleep."

He pondered her answer, brow furrowed. While it wasn't uncommon for people to have carbon monoxide leaks, something about the way she answered him raised the tiny hairs on the back of his neck. "But..."

Resting her head against the headrest, Tessa let out a sigh before answering. "I know Daddy had the furnace checked a few weeks before it happened. He was meticulous about maintaining all the mechanicals around the place. Kept a handwritten calendar in his desk where he'd check off when the cars needed service, and other routine things. The furnace got serviced every winter, and the air conditioning system checked every summer. I didn't believe it when investigators deemed it an accident. Even went so far as to call the company who serviced the equipment. Spoke with the owner. He provided documentation the equipment was in perfect working condition at the time of inspection and servicing."

First thing I'd have done too.

"Do the police suspect it wasn't an accident?"

"Coroner's report showed super-high levels of CO_2 in their systems. The furnace must have been slowly leaking for a few days without them noticing. Mom mentioned she was coming down with the flu. They just—went to sleep and never woke up."

Glancing in the rearview mirror, he pulled over to the

side of the road. Undoing his seatbelt and then hers, he leaned across and pulled Tessa into his arms, held her close, and rocked her gently. Carbon monoxide poisoning was a horrific way for anybody to die, and he regretted making her relive her parents' loss again with his prying questions.

"I'm sorry, Red."

She sniffled against his shoulder. "Not your fault."

"I know, but I shouldn't have pried."

Leaning back, she looked into his eyes, her own swimming with tears. "You didn't. I'm glad I told you. Talking about them is hard, but it's getting easier. I think it hit Beth harder, because of Jamie. Poor little thing, she's growing up with so few memories of her grandparents. She's only three. How much is she going to remember of the two people who adored her?"

She pulled away, and reluctantly he forced his arms to loosen, letting her put distance between them, though it was hard. Red felt right in his embrace, and he wanted to keep her there.

"Kids are resilient. You and your sister will make sure she never forgets her grandparents loved her."

"We're trying. Evan, Jamie's father, still has his mother, so she has one living grandparent."

"Good. Family is important." He reached forward and brushed a long auburn lock behind her ear, his fingertips skimming across her jawline. The softness of her skin felt like silk, and he lingered, running his finger along her jaw again.

Watched her eyes drift closed as she leaned into his touch.

He jerked at the sound of a horn, dragging his attention back to his surroundings, and what he was supposed to be doing—dealing with Jeb Grady's complaint—not almost kissing Red in the front seat of his sheriff's car. Glancing through the window, he spotted his father's car idling beside him, and gave a sheepish grin and a short wave in his direction.

Great, caught by my old man, making out in the front seat of my car. That hasn't happened since I was in my teens.

Douglas motioned for him to roll down the window. "Everything okay, son?"

"Fine, Dad. We were…talking."

From the look on his daddy's face, he knew exactly what they'd almost been doing, and from his grin, his father wasn't opposed to the idea.

"I spotted your car, and thought maybe you'd had some trouble. Since everything's fine, I'll be on my way. Talk to you later, son."

Without another word, Douglas drove away, leaving Rafe leaning his head against the steering wheel, his shoulders shaking. "I am never going to live this down, Red. I suspect he's already on the phone with Momma, telling her how he found us making out on the side of the road."

"But…but, we weren't…"

"Sure as God made little green apples, we would have been if he'd arrived a minute later, darlin'."

"Oh."

"By the time we get back to town, the rest of the Boudreaus will have heard the news too. Don't worry, they won't tell anybody outside the family, but I suspect we're in for a bit of teasing. Some of my brothers have very warped senses of humor."

Pulling back onto the road, he glanced at Red, trying to gauge her reaction. Fingertips against her lips, she stared out the windshield, silent. While he didn't regret stopping and holding her in his arms, he probably should have picked a more secluded spot. Beside him, he heard a sputtering noise, and looked over. Hands covered her face, as she rocked in her seat.

"I'm sorry, Red. I'll make sure nobody says a word. Embarrassing you is the last—"

Before he could finish, peals of laughter spilled from Tessa, the sound joyous and free. "I can't believe your father caught us on the side of the road. Did you see his face? I'm not sure if he was appalled or thrilled."

Rafe knew exactly how Douglas felt. They'd had a long chat the day after the barbecue. He'd confided in his dad he planned on courting Tessa, and Douglas gave his blessing. Not that he needed it, but knowing his father approved went a long way. Finding a woman like Tessa was an unexpected blessing as far as he was concerned. The more time he spent with her, the more things he discovered about her that fascinated and enchanted him. She wasn't perfect, and didn't pretend to be. What she was, was honest, and forthright, and sweet. He liked her—a lot.

"It doesn't bother you? That the whole family will assume we're together?"

Sobering, she looked in his direction, though she didn't quite meet his gaze. "Only if it bothers you, Rafe."

"The only thing bothering me at the moment is I have to get to Jeb Grady's place and deal with his complaint, instead of picking up where we left off."

The prettiest blush stained her cheeks. "Let's go and handle Mr. Grady's problem, and you can buy me the lunch you promised. Then we'll see what happens."

Stomping on the accelerator, Rafe headed for Jeb Grady's farm, his lips curved in a smile. This day was definitely looking up.

CHAPTER FIFTEEN

"Sheriff, I ain't gonna lie. If you don't catch them dadburn kids what's doing this, I ain't gonna be responsible for my actions the next time they trespass on my place."

Tessa watched the older man standing beside Rafe, who was studying the side of the henhouse currently decorated with splashes of color, courtesy of several cans of spray paint, tossed at the base of the coop. Moving closer, he inspected the design, which didn't resemble anything threatening, more like somebody swept their arm in an arch while holding the spray can. Looking at the weather-beaten, wooden structure with its tin roof, Tessa secretly felt the spray paint was a vast improvement in its appearance, but kept her opinion to herself. Exacerbating the temper of the older man wouldn't help the situation.

"Jeb, did you see or hear anything before you found this?" Rafe's hand pointed toward the graffiti-covered henhouse.

"If I'd heard 'em, you'd be hauling their butts to jail right now, instead of standing here jawing at me. It was like this when I came out here to collect the eggs."

"Did you touch anything? Pick up the cans of paint?"

A guilty look passed over Grady's face, while he blustered and postured, trying to divert the attention back to the henhouse. Tessa studied the old farmer closely. Something seemed off with this whole picture, but without all the facts, she didn't want to jump to conclusions. Instead, she kept her lips zipped and stood back, letting Rafe do his job.

"I...um..."

"I'll take that as a yes then." Rafe knelt and picked up the can with the blue lid, his hands wrapped in the plastic gloves he'd retrieved from his car. "I'll bag these up and take them in for fingerprints, but unless the kids caused trouble in the past, they won't have prints on file."

"Well, don't see any reason for you to bother then, Sheriff. Gotta say, it's getting mighty hard to get a good night's sleep around here anymore, what with sitting up, wondering if them good-fer-nothing's are gonna show up and cause me more problems."

"Mr. Grady?"

He turned toward her, pulling a rag out of his back pocket, and running it across his face, which was peppered with sweat. "Yes, ma'am? Whatcha need?"

"I was wondering if I might trouble you for a glass of water?" She cut her gaze toward Rafe, who was standing at her side, and he quirked his brow. Something niggled at the back of her head, a hunch, and maybe if she asked a few leading questions, she might figure out a way to solve Mr. Grady's problems.

"Land's sakes, where are my manners? Come on up to the house, little lady, and I'll get you something right away." She watched him scurry toward the back door of his farmhouse, his scrawny frame making quick work of the distance.

"What's up, Red?" Rafe's hand touched her elbow, as she stepped over a tree root from the huge live oak in the yard. It was enormous, spreading its branches across the entire back porch. The shade felt wonderful. Although the day was only half over, it was already in the mid-nineties, and the weather forecast stated it would be over a hundred by late afternoon.

"I'm not sure, but I have a hunch. Mind playing along for a bit?"

"I've got my own suspicions, but I'm game. Jeb seems to like you."

Tessa smiled. "He's a crusty old curmudgeon, isn't he?"

"What he is, is a pain in my—backside. This is the fourth call out here in as many months."

Pulling open the back door, Rafe motioned her inside, where she was met with blessed coolness. An overhead ceiling fan rotated on a low setting, the windows in the kitchen propped open, pulling the breeze in from outside. Older places like this normally didn't have air conditioning, not unless they'd gone through renovations, and it didn't look like Mr. Grady's home had seen hide-nor-hair of an interior designer, much less a coat of paint in decades. The place was spotlessly clean, dishes stacked in the drainer, and a row of clear glass canisters lining the tiled countertop.

"Here you go, ma'am. I added some ice, since it's blistering outside. Sheriff, fixed you one too." Grady pushed a second glass across the table, and Tessa hid her smile behind the rim of her glass when she noted Rafe only warranted two measly ice cubes, while she had a glass full.

Setting her glass on the wooden tabletop, she watched Jeb Grady putter around the kitchen like a flustered housewife, opening a cabinet and taking down a package of store-bought cookies, and placing several on a plate. Bustling over to the table, he placed it precisely in the center, before lowering himself onto the chair beside Tessa. Rafe stood leaning against the doorjamb between the kitchen and the hallway.

"Mr. Grady, you have a lovely place."

"Thank you, ma'am. Bought it back in sixty-five, right after me and the missus got hitched. Raised our three boys here, but they've all moved to the big city—for their jobs." His expression when he mentioned the big city left a very distinct impression, like it was a bad word leaving an unpleasant aftertaste in his mouth. Glancing around the kitchen, she didn't spot a lot of feminine touches, other than the ruffled curtains above the sink. Faded and yellowed with age, they looked to have been there for a long time.

"The sheriff explained you've been having trouble for

several weeks now. Vandalism like this should never be ignored." She glanced in Rafe's direction, and noted his eye roll. She bit the inside of her cheek to keep from laughing. At least he kept his mouth shut, for the time being.

"Exactly what I tell the sheriff, every time I call. Something's got to be done."

"Especially with them shooting at your barn. Somebody could have been hurt—or worse." Tessa hoped he'd open up and talk, because if her suspicions were right, that's exactly what he needed. Somebody to talk to. Being alone, with no family or friends close by, she couldn't imagine the loneliness. In North Carolina, she'd always had people around, her parents or her sister. Even little Jamie brought joy to her life. Since moving to Texas, she'd made new friends, and kept busy getting ready for school, even meeting all her students and their parents. The activities kept her from feeling isolated or alone.

"Ain't nobody out here to get hurt besides me, ma'am. Besides, I chased 'em off long before the sheriff made it out here." Jeb cut his eyes at Rafe, the corners of his mouth turned down. "Takes them forever to come."

"Jeb, we've had somebody respond to every single call you've placed. Somebody spray painting graffiti on the side of your henhouse isn't precisely an emergency call. I'm here, and you know I'm doing my best to find out who is messing with your farm."

Jeb's whole body seemed to deflate at Rafe's words.

Though she didn't know the older man, it broke her heart to see the life and energy seem to drain away before her eyes.

"Mr. Grady—"

"Call me Jeb, ma'am. No need to be all formal like around here."

She smiled and reacting on impulse, reached out and squeezed his hand. "I was wondering...no, never mind, it's too much to ask."

"Tessa?"

"No, it's okay, Rafe. I was going to ask Mr. Grad— Jeb—if he'd mind my dropping by to ask some questions about farming. But I realized he's so busy, running this farm on his own, he doesn't have time to deal with my ignorance."

"Nonsense." Jeb's chest puffed out like he was cock of the walk in a pen full of hens. "You got questions about farming, ain't nobody in this county can teach you like me."

She felt Rafe's gaze boring into hers, and she watched the light of understanding dawn, and he gave her a brilliant smile. He'd caught on to what she'd been trying to impart in a roundabout way without hurting the old guy's feelings. How sad was it, to be all alone, with nobody to talk to, unless you called the sheriff on some half-baked excuse, for a little human contact?

"He's right, Tessa. There is nobody in Shiloh Springs and beyond who knows more about what it takes to run a farm than Jeb Grady. He's practically a legend around these parts."

"But I wouldn't want to be a pest. Coming from the city, I don't have the first clue about what it takes to grow crops, or tend to animals. As far as I know, corn and carrots show up in the grocery store, ready to eat."

Jeb stood and moved to the counter, grabbing the water pitcher and refilling her half-empty glass. "Most folks don't realize what real farming is all about. You want to learn? I'll teach ya. Come out any time, Ms. Tessa, and I'll put you to work. There ain't a finer feeling than sticking your hands into rich black soil, planting seeds, and watching things grow."

"Are you sure, Jeb? I know how busy you are. Rafe was telling me on the way here how much he admires your expertise and skill."

I did? Rafe mouthed the words and she winked at him when Jeb wasn't looking.

"Don't worry, Jeb, I'm going to make sure those teenagers don't mess with you anymore. Tell you what, how about this weekend I come over and help you repaint the hen house, and get rid of the graffiti?"

"I'd like that, Sheriff. I'd like it a lot."

CHAPTER SIXTEEN

Pulling into Tessa's drive, Rafe cut the engine and climbed from his cruiser, walking around to open her door. He still couldn't believe she'd figured out Jeb Grady's problem, having only met the man a few hours earlier. A wave of guilt tightened in his gut. How had he missed all the signs? He'd know the older man for most of his adult life, had answered numerous calls for the sheriff's office, and never once had it occurred to him the old guy might be so lonely, he'd risk getting arrested, just to have somebody to talk to.

"Thanks for dinner."

Another flash of guilt hit. His plans for taking Red to lunch had gone sideways. Instead they'd spent several hours with Jeb, only leaving when he'd complained he needed to get up early the next morning or the chores wouldn't get done. They'd ended up at Daisy's Diner, and while the food there was always great, he'd planned on taking her someplace a little more romantic. Plus, she didn't get her Tex-Mex.

He started to answer, but her darkened front porch caught his eye and he stopped, placing a hand on her arm.

Something didn't feel right. He knew the front porch light automatically kicked on. It was the type attached to a motion sensor, because he'd installed it himself. It should have turned on when he pulled into the drive. Instead, the yard was painted with a wash of moonlight—no artificial light except for the streetlight half a block away.

Glancing across the street, he noted dim lights through the front curtains, which meant the power wasn't off. A tingle raced down his spine, and he whispered, "Wait here."

"What's wrong?"

"Probably nothing, but your light should have kicked on. Stay here and let me check. Maybe the bulb went out." Slipping up the steps, he kept his footfalls silent. Nothing looked disturbed, yet his cop instincts screamed danger with a capital D. Something was wrong. Using the edge of his shirt, he twisted the doorknob and the front door slid open.

"I locked it."

He bit back a curse. He hadn't heard her follow him onto the porch. Maybe he was losing his edge. "Thought I told you to wait."

"Hate to tell you this, Sheriff, but you're not the boss of me."

Yep, that statement totally deserved the eye roll.

"Red, let me do my job. Do not move from this spot." Since he'd been on duty all day, he was still in his uniform, and his hand flicked open the snap on his holster, freeing his service weapon. He eased the door open, enough to slide through, and allowed his eyes to adjust to the darkened interior. Taking two steps into the living room, his eyes landed on the overturned furniture first, then the contents of shelves tossed onto the floor. Stuffing and batting spilled from the sofa through large slashes. He'd been a cop long enough to know somebody had tossed Red's place.

Within minutes, he'd checked the entire house, finding the same thing in every room. The drawers emptied and scattered, furniture upended or broken.

The bedroom and office took the brunt of the damage, with the bedding and padded headboard sliced open and ripped. Pulling out his phone, he dialed the station and requested the crime scene investigators as well as the on-duty deputy hightail it to Tessa's house.

When he came out of the office, he glanced toward the front door, and spotted Tessa standing there, a fist pressed against her mouth. Long strides brought him to her in seconds, and he pulled her into his arms. He could feel her body tremble against his, and he ran his hand soothingly down her spine, offering her comfort.

"Why? I don't understand—who would do something like this?"

"Sweetheart, we may not be the big city, but we still have the same problems. Most likely it was somebody looking for money or something they could sell for some quick cash." He cupped her cheek, forcing her to meet his gaze. "I've got my people coming to take fingerprints and collect any evidence we can find. Do you think you can take a look around—tell me if anything's missing?"

With his hand still against her back, he felt her spine straightening, one disk at a time, until she stood ramrod straight and stiff. He could only imagine the gamut of emotions racing through her. This was a violation, emotional and physical, and one he could only stand by and offer support, at least until they caught whoever did it. Then he'd make sure they paid, even if he had to take it out of their hides the old-fashioned way.

He watched her step gingerly through the miasma of papers, broken glass, and the spewed innards of her sofa and two stuffed chairs, eyes darting from one end of the room to the other. Heard her ragged indrawn breath when she noted the shattered glass figurine on the floor, its delicate beauty forever destroyed. His instincts, the ones all cops have, screamed this didn't look like a random act of violence. It was too destructive, almost vengeful. This seemed...personal.

He trailed her from room to room, until she stood at the doorway leading to her bedroom, her hand at her throat. Everything in him clamored to grab her up, take her away from all this destruction, the ugliness, but he couldn't. He needed to do his job, which meant being detached and analytical—the last thing he felt around Red.

A sound drew his gaze to the front door, where he spotted Dusty and the crime scene investigation team. Dusty nodded once, and directed the crew toward the living room.

They were a good team, and did their job well, but right now he wasn't focused on gathering evidence. No, he was focused on the woman standing beside him.

"I don't understand. Rafe, this doesn't make any sense. If they were looking for something to sell, they wouldn't have done this much damage." She turned to face him, her eyes swimming with tears. "Why would somebody hate me this much?"

The hell with it. Taking her in his arms, he led her out of the house and to his car, opening the door, and easing her onto the seat. He didn't know what to tell her; he didn't have a clue why somebody trashed her place. In the short time she'd been in Shiloh Springs, he doubted she'd made any enemies. And his gut told him this wasn't some punks out for a quick fix.

"I promise, Red, we'll figure out who did this, and send them away for a long time." Reaching up, he framed her face with his hands, tilting it up until she met his eyes. "Trust me, sweetheart. I won't let anything happen to you."

Before he could say anything else, a car pulled into the drive behind his, high beams illuminating everything. Shielding his eyes, he recognized his mother's car. Word traveled fast in Shiloh Springs, and he suspected Dusty probably called her as soon as he'd called the station. Not only was Ms. Patti the landlord on record for the property, but she'd taken a personal interest in Tessa—had right from the start.

"Oh sugar, are you okay?" He moved out of the way before his momma bowled him over. The scent of her perfume gave him a sense of peace, and he knew she'd take care of Red, smother her with the loving warmth only a mother can. Turning to him, his mother gave him an angry glare, one he knew wasn't directed at him personally, but at the situation. He didn't blame her. He was itching to get his hands on whoever broke in and turned Tessa's life upside down.

"I'm fine." Tessa's words came out whispered. Walking around to his trunk, he popped it and lifted out the emergency blanket he kept in there. Placing it around her shoulders, he watched her snuggle into its depths. Though it was still in the nineties, he noted her shivering. Definitely shock.

"Is she done here?" His momma looked at him, while her hand continued its soothing caress of Tessa's hair. Over and over, the soft petting motion seemed automatic, and he watched Tessa's shivers slowly diminish. Trust his momma to know exactly what to do. Then again, she'd been dealing with eleven boys and one spirited tomboy for a long time, and her motherly instincts had kicked into overdrive. "I'm gonna take her home with me."

From her tone, he knew there was no arguing. When Ms. Patti got that no-nonsense quality in her voice, there wasn't a person in Shiloh Springs who'd gainsay her. "Good idea, Momma. I have to stay here, and finish processing the scene, but I'll—"

"Come by in the morning." She nodded her head to the side, indicating she wanted to talk to him privately. Walking a few feet away, she continued. "Rafe, I know you're going to have questions, but can't they wait until tomorrow? Right now, I think she'll do better with a hot cup of tea and maybe a shoulder to cry on." Reaching forward, she brushed her thumb along his cheek, a gesture she'd done a thousand times when he'd been growing up. "And I know you want to be that shoulder, but I don't think she's ready—not yet at any rate. You do your job, and find out who did this. I'll do mine, and take care of your girl, okay?"

Without a word, he pulled his mother into his arms, hugging her tight. Trust her to know exactly what needed doing, and to get it done. She was right too, blast it. Tessa was in shock, fragile and vulnerable. And probably feeling violated in a way only another woman would understand.

"Take care of her, Momma. If she needs anything, call me and I'll be there."

Reaching up, she patted his cheek. "I know. You are a good boy, Rafael."

Walking to the car, he squatted beside Tessa, still seated in his squad car. "Red, Momma's gonna take you home with her, while I stay here and figure out who broke into your house. She'll take good care of you. But you need anything, you have her call me and I'll be there faster than you can blink, okay?"

Her red-rimmed eyes met his. "Okay. I…thank you."

The blanket slipped off one shoulder, and he reached out and gently lifted it to cover her again. Her tentative smile nearly broke his heart. The day which had begun with so much promise had turned into an unmitigated mess, but he'd find a way to make things right again. Bring back her sense of safety and hope.

"Come on, sweetheart, let's leave Rafe to do his job, and we'll go home and have a nice cup of tea and a hot bath. How's that sound?"

Tessa stood, placing the blanket onto the car seat, and took a step away before turning back to him. "Find out who did this, Rafe."

"I will, darlin'. I promise."

CHAPTER SEVENTEEN

Wrapped in a warm bathrobe, and sipping hot tea, Tessa sat with her feet drawn up beneath her in the overstuffed arm chair. Wet hair hung loosely over her shoulders, evidence of the hot shower she'd taken upon arriving at the Big House. Ms. Patti met her at the door when she emerged, guiding her to the living room, and handing her the cup of hot tea, laced with a liberal dose of something strong.

"Feeling better?"

"Yes, thank you. It was all a bit overwhelming, but it's starting to sink in. I don't understand why somebody would destroy my home. The more I think about it, it doesn't feel like a random break in. Somebody looking for money wouldn't take a knife to the sofa or the chair—or my bed."

She hated the way her voice cracked on the last words. Now the shock was wearing off, white hot anger coursed through her like a volcano, the pressure building and bubbling to the surface until she felt like she'd explode. Nobody had the right to invade her home, much less destroy her things. Most of the furniture had come with the house—

she'd rented it furnished—but the things she'd brought with her held sentimental value and were irreplaceable. *At least to me.*

"I admit we don't see a lot of robberies in Shiloh Springs. Not like you'd expect in the bigger cities. Our son, Antonio, lives in Dallas. I don't think a day goes by I'm not concerned about his safety, though I'd never tell him. He loves living there, and he loves his job. So, I've learned to keep my feelings to myself. When something like this happens…"

"It makes you feel like you've lost something special. That feeling of safety in your own home." Tessa ran a hand through her hair, feeling the curls springing to life as it started drying. "The thing I can't seem to wrap my head around? Why? I'm not rich. Other than a couple of pieces of jewelry belonging to my mother, I don't own anything worth taking."

Ms. Patti placed a small plate with three chocolate chip cookies on it on the table by Tessa's chair. "You're still fairly new in Shiloh Springs. Somebody desperate enough might figure you'd be an easier mark than one of the locals. Honestly, who knows? I don't think like a criminal, so haven't got a real clue how their mind works."

Tessa took another sip of tea, before nibbling on one of the cookies. The brown sugar and chocolate melted on her tongue. No way were these bought at any store. They reminded her of the cookies her granny made when she and Beth were little.

Her head lifted at the sound of the front door, and Brody walked in, bending low to press a kiss against his mother's cheek. His bright blue eyes studied her, concern written on his face. "I heard about what happened. You okay?"

Nodding, she answered, "I'm fine. Thankfully, I wasn't at home when whoever it was broke in."

He perched on the arm of the sofa next to his mother. "I spoke with Rafe a few minutes ago. They're nearly finished, and he's going to make sure the house is locked up tight when the investigative team finishes." With a devilish wink, he reached across, snagged one of the cookies off her plate and bit into it, his eyes alight with laughter.

"Brody Boudreau, you know better!"

"You know I can't resist your cookies, Momma." Sobering, he turned back to Tessa. "Is there anything you need? I can run by your place before they lock up."

"I can't think of anything, but thank you for offering."

"No problem. I just got off duty, and heard what happened. Swung by your house before I headed here." He turned toward his mother. "Rafe said most of the furniture is a total loss. Why don't you use the stuff I've got in storage?" When Tessa started to interrupt, he raised his hand, and continued. "It's gathering dust inside one of those paid storage places. I'd much rather you get some use out of it. No, don't protest. Your place came furnished, and it's the least I can do, until you get some new stuff."

"Thank you, son. That'll help a lot, and give me time to

contact Darrell Johnson about filing an insurance claim, and getting replacements."

"It's settled then. Once Rafe gives the all clear, I'll grab a couple guys and we'll get you fixed up good as new, Tessa."

She felt tears welling in her eyes. The Boudreaus had gone out of their way to make her feel welcome in Shiloh Springs from the moment she'd arrived. Well, except for her first debacle with Rafe. Now here they were again, coming to her rescue.

"Ah, don't cry, Tessa. Everything's going to be okay."

She sniffled then chuckled, brushing at her eyes. "I know. You've all been so kind. Taking me in, helping me..."

"That's what family does." Ms. Patti stood and wrapped an arm around Brody's middle. "Finish your tea, while I walk this hooligan out to his truck."

"Guess I've overstayed my welcome," Brody joked. "Good night, Tessa. See you tomorrow."

Tessa stared at the cup of tea between her hands. Taking another sip, she felt the warmth spread through her, seep into her very bones. She couldn't stop thinking about walking in the door, and finding nothing but devastation. Leaning against the back of the chair, she closed her eyes, determined to find an answer.

After saying goodnight to her son, Patti stopped in the

opening to the living room. A tiny smile tugged at the corners of her lips. Tessa sat curled in the easy chair, fast asleep. Picking up the crocheted throw her mother made, she gently draped it across Tessa's shoulders.

Poor thing definitely had an eventful day. Douglas had called earlier, right after he'd caught Rafe and Tessa canoodling on the side of the road. She could still hear him snickering as he recounted the tale. Her son was smitten with the pretty new school teacher, and if she wasn't mistaken, more than halfway in love with her. And if she wasn't mistaken, Tessa felt the same.

Walking into the kitchen, she pulled out her cell and dialed Rafe.

"Momma? How's Tessa?"

"Tessa is fast asleep in your daddy's chair. I called to check on you."

There was a pause, long enough she was afraid he wouldn't answer. Then he sighed. "Somebody did a real number on her place."

"Son, I didn't ask about her place. How are *you* holding up?"

Rafe gave a ragged laugh, the sound brittle and hollow. "Honestly? I don't know. I'm doing my best to remain professional and treat this like any other crime scene. Except it's not. Scenarios keep playing in my head, over and over. What if she'd been home? What if I hadn't noticed the motion detector not coming on and she walked into that whole mess alone? What if they'd still been there, and I couldn't help her?"

"You care about her." It wasn't a question.

"Yeah. Kind of snuck up on me, and it's way too soon to call it the L word, but she means a lot to me."

"If she's important to you, then we'll have to make sure nothing happens to her. When you're finished, go home and try to get some sleep. We'll take good care of Tessa, I promise."

"Momma, I…"

Patti glanced through the opening leading from the kitchen to the living room, separated only by a hallway, studying the woman they were talking about. "I know, son. It'll work out, you'll see."

Over the line, she heard voices in the background, knew he needed to deal with his people, get the job done. But he was her son, *her first child*, which made it much harder knowing he was in pain, and there wasn't a thing she could do about it.

"I've gotta run. Tell Tessa I'll see her tomorrow."

"I will. Good night, Rafe."

Standing in the doorway, she watched Tessa sleep. Despite her repose, a worry line appeared between her brows, as if she couldn't relax even in sleep. Shaking her head, Patti walked to the front door and did something she never thought she'd have to do in Shiloh Springs.

She turned the lock.

CHAPTER EIGHTEEN

Tessa walked through the front door of her house the next morning, staring in disbelief. The scene from the previous night might well have been a bad dream, because no trace of the devastation remained. The broken and unusable furniture had been removed, the papers picked up and stacked neatly.

"Good. The boys got everything tidied up." Ms. Patti walked past her into the kitchen, and set her purse on the table. "Lucas, Joshua, and Shiloh should be here any time with the stuff from Brody's storage locker."

"Ms. Patti, I'm speechless." Tessa moved her arm in an arc, indicating the living room. "Last night, this was a total disaster. I thought I'd come home, and spend the day trying to deal with the mess."

Ms. Patti squeezed her shoulder. "Neighbors help each other. At least we do in Shiloh Springs. Between you and me, though, I can't guarantee my boys put everything back exactly where you had it. But you've got time to get things squared away." She grinned and winked. "The thing about having eleven boys—you've always got more than enough hanging around to get things done."

"I can't imagine having a house filled with so many kids."

"Well, sugar, we didn't have them all at once. Rafe tell how he came to live with us?"

She nodded. "Some of it. I think he might have skimmed over the more salient details."

"Come on, we might as well get comfortable, at least until my boys get here with the furniture." They made their way into the kitchen, and Tessa headed straight for the refrigerator. Pulling it open, she noted the half full pitcher of lemonade she'd made the morning before. Pouring two glasses, she handed one to Ms. Patti before sitting across from the older woman.

"Would you mind telling me? About Rafe, I mean."

"Rafe was our first." Tessa heard the nostalgic note in Ms. Patti's voice, a wistful expression crossing her face. "Douglas and I tried for a long time to get pregnant. My OB/GYN said it would take a miracle for me to conceive, and even if I did, the chances were slim I'd carry to full term."

"That's awful." What can you say when somebody tells you about a painful chapter in their life? Tessa couldn't imagine the sorrow and grief Ms. Patti and Douglas must have felt. When Ms. Patti reached across the table and squeezed her hand, she realized her expression must have given her away.

"Once we got past the shock, we decided to leave everything in God's hands. We talked about adoption, maybe getting a surrogate. But like everything else in life, when you start making plans, the world creates havoc around you, derailing everything you accomplish."

Tessa knew the feeling first hand, especially with the loss of her parents. Life took unexpected twists and turns, and she never knew what was coming next. "I get it. I had my life planned out too, then things spun out of control, and here I am in Shiloh Springs. But, please—tell me more—about how you got Rafe."

"After Douglas got out of the Army, he wanted to move back to Shiloh Springs. This is his home. It's in his blood. Where he grew up, and where the family's ranch is, so we came back. His brother ran the ranch itself, which was fine with Douglas. He didn't have an interest in raising cattle. Anyway, I'll skip ahead a few years. Douglas started his construction company, and did volunteer work for the fire department whenever he could. He loved being involved with the community, though they didn't get a lot of calls. Shiloh Springs was a lot smaller then. One night, he responded to a bad car wreck. The woman driving killed, but the boy was still alive but trapped inside."

"Rafe?" Tessa said his name quietly, not wanting Ms. Patti to stop telling the story.

"Yes. Douglas said it was one of the worst wrecks he'd ever seen. They had to use the Jaws of Life to cut the roof and the door off, to get to him. To this day, I still remember his voice when he told me about the wreck, and them pulling the boy free. He had a large gash on his head, and was covered with so much blood they couldn't tell if he had any other injuries. When they loaded him onto a gurney, he latched onto Douglas' hand, and begged him not to leave him. Douglas said Rafe gripped so tight, he nearly cut off the circulation. Poor child, he already knew his mother was dead."

Tessa walked over to the sink, and stood staring out the window, picturing the scene in her mind. To have endured so much, when he was still a child. "How old was he?"

"Eleven."

"I can't even…" She broke off, because what could she say?

"Douglas rode in the ambulance with him to the hospital, held his hand the entire way. Rafe clung to Douglas like he was his only lifeline in a world gone crazy. My husband stayed at the hospital the entire night. Never left Rafe's side. He called me the next morning, told me to come to the hospital. When I walked into Rafe's room, Douglas was sitting in a chair beside the bed, sound asleep, still clinging to that little boy's hand. I knew, before he ever spoke a single word, we had a special child about to become part of us— part of our family."

Tessa turned toward Ms. Patti, hearing the catch in her voice. "He is very lucky to have you."

RAFE

She shook her head. "No, sugar, we're the lucky ones. It wasn't easy. First, we had to get emergency certification to become foster parents." Laughing, she added, "We were totally clueless. Fortunately, Douglas' captain at the fire station knew a wonderful social worker, who helped facilitate the process and we were approved, so by the time Rafe could leave the hospital, we were ready for him. Well, as ready as two people can be when a traumatized eleven-year-old is dropped into their laps."

"He's a Boudreau, though. Did you formally adopt him?"

Ms. Patti huffed out a laugh at her words. "I'd have adopted him in a heartbeat, so would Douglas. Except we couldn't, because his father is still alive."

Shock spilled through Tessa at the other woman's words. Rafe mentioned his father when telling her about his past, how he'd abused and murdered his mother, and was serving life in prison. It didn't make sense. If Douglas and Ms. Patti hadn't adopted him, how was he a Boudreau?

"I won't talk about his biological father. That's up to Rafe to tell you—or not. But my boy is a Boudreau through-and-through. He might not be our blood, but he owns every bit of our hearts."

Tessa watched Ms. Patti struggle against tears, and felt a knot in the pit of her gut. She hadn't wanted to upset her friend, and a wave of guilt swamped her. "I'm sorry, I didn't mean to upset you."

"Hush, girl. You didn't upset me. Sometimes the memories can be a tad overwhelming. Where was I? Oh, right, Rafe. He lived with us until he turned eighteen, when he graduated from high school and prepared to go to A&M. I was so proud of him. He got a full scholarship. You've never seen anybody work so hard for something. Anyway, right before he left, he sat down with Douglas and me. Said he had something to show us. Then he handed his father a set of legal papers." Ms. Patti closed her eyes, the slightest smile on her lips. The glow of happiness radiating from her was nearly palpable, along with a sense of contentment.

"What kind of papers?" Tessa couldn't resist asking.

"He'd gone through the whole process of legally changing his name to Boudreau. Never said a word to either of us, so we didn't have a clue what he intended. Said while he'd never turn his back on his birth mother and how important she'd been in his life, we were his family. The papers reflected the change in his legal name to Rafael Felipe Alvarado Boudreau." She paused for a second, a faraway look in her gaze. "His mother's maiden name was Alvarado."

Tessa's chest tightened with so much emotion she could barely breathe. She'd found Rafe to be an honorable and caring man. Still, the actions of an eighteen-year-old barely out of school, delineated him, shaped and honed him into the strong and compassionate man she was secretly afraid she was falling in love with. The act of someone confident in himself, with a whole heart filled with love to give. A true testament to what Douglas and Ms. Patti taught him. "That's amazing."

"He's amazing. I'm going to tell you something I've never told another living soul, and don't you repeat it."

Tessa placed her hand on her heart. "I promise."

"Rafe left that night to go meet up with his brothers at the diner. They'd planned a big going away celebration, just the guys. My husband isn't an overtly emotional man. Stoic, irascible, he's generous to a fault and he'll give you his last dime without a single question. He's as big as a mountain, but after Rafe left that night, Douglas broke down and cried. I held my husband in my arms while he wept like a baby, because he loves that boy more than his own life. Regardless of the circumstances which brought Rafe into our lives, he's *ours*."

It was the proverbial last straw. Tessa walked around the table, and wrapped her arms around Ms. Patti's shoulders. Whether the other woman knew it or not, she'd given Tessa an unguarded look into the past of a man who was slowly making a place for himself in her life and her heart. While the thought should have scared her, it didn't.

"Thank you for sharing with me."

With a sigh, Ms. Patti pulled back and met Tessa's gaze. "You're a nice woman, and I like you. And I think my son likes you too. But," she paused to emphasize the seriousness of her words, "you hurt him, and you'll answer to me."

"I have no intention of hurting Rafe. I...care about

him."

At the sound of voices from outside, Tessa straightened. She stared as several Boudreau men came through her front door. Lucas was first, holding the door wide, while Joshua and another man wrestled a butterscotch-colored leather sofa through her front door. Hair dark as a raven's wing spilled free across wide shoulders. When he looked up, she met a pair of startling blue eyes. The combination gave him a slightly exotic look.

Giving her a lopsided grin, he asked, "Where do you want this?" He nodded toward the sofa, and she pointed toward the living room, still staring. She'd seen a lot of handsome guys, but Shiloh Boudreau took her breath away. The man could easily grace the cover of GQ. Though she was attracted to Rafe, she wasn't blind, and Shiloh Boudreau embodied masculinity personified. A glorious specimen of masculinity. He had the kind of face her mother used to call angel-kissed.

Ms. Patti strolled in from the kitchen, and nudged Tessa out of the way with a hip bump. "I'll take care of this, sugar." With the air of a drill sergeant, she directed the men, and soon her living room and bedroom contained the replacement furniture Brody had offered, substitutes for the items the burglar destroyed.

"Hey, Momma, you in there?"

Ms. Patti whipped around at the sound the voice from outside, before turning to glare at Shiloh. "*Ridge is home?*

Why didn't you tell me?"

He shrugged. "He wanted it to be a surprise."

Tessa glanced up when another man strode through the front door, and knew her jaw hung open. Looking at Ms. Patti, she whispered, "There are two of them?"

The other woman chuckled. "Twins."

The newcomer winked at her, and Tessa's hands flew to her cheeks. Caught staring, heat flooded her cheeks when Shiloh chuckled.

"Meet my brother, Ridge."

"A pleasure, Ms. Tessa." She watched Ridge envelope Ms. Patti in a bear hug, lifting her clear off the floor and spinning her around. Her joyous laugh spread through the living room.

Tessa found herself fascinated with all the Boudreau men. Each seemed to have an interesting tale connecting them to Douglas and Ms. Patti, and she'd love to pursue Shiloh and Ridge's, but it would have to wait for another time and place. At the moment, her little house overflowed with Boudreaus, and she hadn't even offered them anything to eat or drink. Where were the southern manners her mother drilled into her since she'd been big enough to tie on an apron?

"I've got iced tea, lemonade, coffee and soda. There's also cinnamon coffee cake and brownies." Glancing around at the men, she decided formality wouldn't do. "Follow me to the kitchen, guys, and help yourselves."

Minutes later, she was down a gallon of iced tea, two coffee cakes and a plateful of iced brownies. She'd have to make sure Jill got an extra big thank you, because she'd stopped by earlier and dropped off the treats, expecting them to last Tessa a while in her freezer. Of course, that was before the Boudreau hoard descended.

"Best brownies I've ever eaten, no offense, Momma." Shiloh popped the last bite in his mouth. Ridge nodded his agreement.

"Wish I could take the credit," Tessa handed out a stack of napkins, watching the men chow down on the sweets. "Jill dropped those off this morning."

"Jill Monroe?" Ms. Patti's brow rose with her question, and Tessa nodded.

"First the cake, and now these goodies. I definitely need to have a chat with Jill." Grabbing the huge bag Ms. Patti never seemed to be without, she dug out her cellphone and made a quick notation, a mysterious smile curving her lips. A shiver skittered down Tessa's spine. She didn't ever want Ms. Patti coming after her with that particular expression.

"Anything else you need, Momma? Otherwise, I've got some stuff I need to get done while I'm here." Ridge stood and tossed his napkin in the trash, before pulling his mother into an embrace.

"Call your father. He's been worried about you."

"I'm planning on stopping by the job site this afternoon anyway. Thought I'd surprise him."

"He'll love that." She hugged him before running her hand over his hair. "I'm so glad you're home."

"Me too."

Tessa's eyes welled at the depth of emotion streaming between Ms. Patti and Ridge. After talking with Rafe at the well in his mother's garden, she'd learned all the Boudreau men weren't the biological children of Douglas and Patti Boudreau, though even a blind person could see that didn't matter. This woman loved all her children. It didn't matter she hadn't carried them within her body—they were *hers*. Her respect and admiration of the woman grew with every passing day. If she could be half the woman Patti Boudreau was, she'd count herself fortunate.

Ms. Patti pulled away from Ridge, and looped the handle of her bag over her shoulder. "Tessa, honey, is there anything else you need?"

"No, I think you've all done more than enough. Please thank Brody again for loaning me his furniture. I'm thankful I don't have to rush around trying to find replacement pieces for everything that got destroyed."

"Hush, girl, it wasn't your fault. Besides, your rental agreement would have handled everything." Her gaze swept the kitchen, landing on each of her sons. "I expect to see you all at the Big House tonight for dinner." She turned back to Tessa. "That includes you. Rafe will pick you up."

"Really, Ms. Patti, he doesn't..." Her words trailed off at Ms. Patti's raised brow. She swallowed back the rest of her protest. "Yes, ma'am."

Ms. Patti chuckled, and patted Tessa's shoulder. "Right answer. See you tonight."

She left, which left Tessa in a kitchen with four Boudreau men and about a million questions. Maybe if she played her cards right, she might be able to get a few of those questions answered. Putting her hands on her hips, she let her gaze meet each Boudreau.

"Anybody still hungry? I've got lasagna."

When all four hands raised, she chuckled. Sometimes guys were just too easy.

CHAPTER NINETEEN

Tessa looked up from the paper she was grading, and found her friend Jill standing in the doorway, a huge grin on her face. They'd made arrangements the night before to meet after school ended for the day. More than ready for a break, she grinned at her friend, whose barely restrained excitement evident in the happy dance she was doing in the open doorway.

"Did you bring it?" Jill's question made Tessa smile even wider.

She held up the family recipe book, its worn brown leather soft against her fingertips. "As promised."

"Awesome! I've been craving those chicken and dumplings your mother made. I swear, even though I've eaten them at dozens of restaurants, nobody made them like she did."

A small pang of grief filled Tessa at the mention of her mother, because the loss was still too fresh. Several months wasn't nearly enough time to forget a lifetime of memories, but the sharp, overwhelming grief had begun fading, becoming more tolerable. Leaving home for a year and taking this job in Shiloh Springs seemed to put things into better perspective and eased the ache of loss. Though she missed her parents, and probably always would, the aching void lessened a little more each day.

"I marked the page so you can write it down." Handing the book to her friend, she chuckled when Jill snatched it from her hand. The avaricious look on Jill's face was priceless.

"I've got you now, my pretty." Her cackling laugh imitated the witch from The Wizard of Oz, as she stroked her hand across the embossed leather cover, before her expression turned serious. "Tessa, you're lucky to have this. In my family, dinner usually meant fast food and pizza most nights. Home cooking at my house was as likely as finding the holy grail."

"My mom loved cooking. Especially those recipes." She pointed at the book Jill held clutched to her chest. "Though you'll see with some of the older recipes, the measurements aren't very precise. A dash of this and a pinch of that. Kinda subjective."

Jill's hand ran across the leather binding in a loving caress. "Isn't that part of the fun? Experimenting and figuring out what works, what tastes good. It's how I do it with my baking. You add a little bit of a certain ingredient, and voila, end up with something amazing."

Tessa chuckled. "And sometimes you end up with wasabi-flavored cupcakes, instead of mint chocolate, because *somebody* picked up the wrong bottle." She couldn't help teasing Jill about her massive baking fail, which had made their house stink for days.

"Sheesh, it was one time."

"Fortunately, you've gotten better since then. Look at the cake you sent for the Boudreau barbecue. Everybody loved it."

A wistful look crossed Jill's face, before quickly disappearing. "Glad they liked it."

Tessa stood and stretched. It had been a long day, though she loved her new class. Deep in her heart, she knew she'd been born to teach. Helping the kids, seeing the joy light their faces when they got the answer right, made her feel like she'd found her calling.

"You got a paper and pen I can borrow?" Jill's question tugged her back into the here and now. "I want to write this down, so I can stop at the grocery on the way home. Since tomorrow's Saturday, I'll have lots of time to make a big pot to last all week."

"Top drawer on the right."

Jill flipped the book open to the marked page, and began furiously writing, her brow creased in concentration. Tessa knew better than to say anything until she'd finished. When Jill focused on a project, nothing short of an atomic bomb blast could distract her.

Maybe she should take a leaf out of Jill's book, and make her own pot of chicken and dumplings. Along with some homemade bread, it would make a nice, comforting meal to share with a certain sheriff.

Before she could change her mind, she picked up her phone and texted Rafe, inviting him for dinner the next night. Almost immediately, she got back a yes and a smiling emoji.

"What's put that look on your face? Jill's tone was teasing. "Or should I say who? Maybe a tall, dark, and handsome sheriff?"

"I invited Rafe to dinner tomorrow night."

"Yes!"

"Don't get so excited, it's only dinner."

Jill studied her intently, and she barely resisted the urge to squirm. "And how many times have you and the good sheriff shared meals recently, hmm?"

"A couple?"

"Girlfriend, you're living in a small town now. *Everybody* knows your business. I could probably ask five people walking down the street how many times you've had lunch or dinner with Rafe, and they could tell me the precise number. So, don't kid a kidder. Are things serious between you?"

Tessa sighed and reached for the recipe book, stroking her fingers lovingly over the cover. "I don't know, Jill. I like him, but after Trevor, I'm not ready to even think about getting into a relationship with anybody."

"Trevor is a jerk and you're well rid of him." Jill gathered up the recipe she'd written and tucked it into her purse. "It's Friday night. Why don't we head over to Daisy's for dinner and girl talk? I haven't seen nearly enough of you since you moved to Shiloh Springs." When Tessa started to refuse, Jill grabbed Tessa's purse and thrust it toward her. "Here. I'm not taking no for an answer—unless you already have plans with Rafe?"

"No. I planned on spending tonight grading these papers, and maybe watching a little TV."

"Then it's settled. You're having dinner with me." Jill's grin was infectious and Tessa found herself responding.

"Okay." She glanced down at the recipe book in her hand. It was too big to fit in her purse. Shrugging, she yanked open the bottom drawer of her desk, and tossed it inside. She'd pick it up later, before she headed to the grocery store, because she didn't want to leave it in her car while she was at the diner. If something happened to it, she'd never forgive herself.

"Awesome!" Jill linked her arm through Tessa's. "You can fill me in on everything—starting with you dating Mr. Hot Sheriff."

Finding a table at Daisy's Diner proved easier said than done. They'd waited outside on the sidewalk lining Main Street for almost twenty minutes before Daisy had snagged them a table. The culinary heart of Shiloh Springs, especially on a Friday night, the place was packed wall-to-wall. Teenagers sat clustered in groups with their pals or significant others, their raucous laughter filling the air. Couples came in for date night, with a lot of hand holding and cuddling in the booths.

Since moving to Shiloh Springs, more than once she'd found herself sitting at the long red Formica counter, chatting with Daisy, who ran the place. They'd hit it off right away, since they both shared a similar background. While Tessa had relocated to Shiloh Springs for the school year to fill in, Daisy had left everything behind to help her uncle run the place after he'd suffered a stroke.

Since it was a Friday night, the joint was jumping, and she felt lucky they'd made it through the doors without an even longer wait. Still, the delay gave her and Jill a chance to chat, and catch up on everything from the past week.

"Mind if we join you?"

Tessa looked into the smiling faces of Ms. Patti and Serena, standing by their table. She waved a hand at the two open chairs. "Of course, we'd love it."

With a grateful smile, Serena flung herself into the chair opposite hers, brushing tendrils of hair away from her face, while Ms. Patti slid onto the other empty seat and gave a contented sigh.

"You wouldn't believe the day I've had." Serena grabbed the glass of ice water as the waitress placed it on the table, and gulped half of it without coming up for air. "You may not know this, but I'm going to clue you in to something I've recently discovered." She paused for dramatic effect before adding, "People suck."

Tessa chuckled at her new friend's scowl. "Would that be people in general, or any one person in particular?" She waggled her brows, and Serena gave her a one-fingered salute. "Like that, is it?"

Serena leaned back in her chair, making a growly sound in the back of her throat. "I have been busting my backside, bending over backward to find the perfect location for a client, until I feel like a pretzel trying to accommodate everything he wants. Talk about picky...no matter what I chose, it wasn't right. Not enough light. Too many windows. Not enough windows. He wanted three stories instead of two. No new construction. Oh, wait, maybe new construction would work." Lifting her glass, she ran it against her forehead with a sigh. "Then today, after I've spent weeks looking for the perfect place for his store, he decides Shiloh Springs isn't the right location anymore, and he is going to look elsewhere."

"I'm sorry, Serena. Sometimes life stinks." Jill reached out and wrapped an arm around Serena's shoulders, giving them a quick squeeze. "It's his loss. He obviously doesn't have a brain in his head, or he'd know Shiloh Springs is the best place in the world."

"She's right," Tessa added. "I love it here. Anybody who

thinks it's not great is a baboon's butt."

She grinned and began thumping Ms. Patti on the back, since she'd taken a sip of her water when Tessa made her remark, and promptly started choking. Waving a hand in front of her face, she caught her breath. "A baboon's butt? That's the best you can do, Tessa?"

"Well, I could have said worse, but there are kids here, and I don't want to corrupt their innocent little ears." She pasted on a demure expression and batted her lashes, assuming such a phony sweet expression it didn't fool anybody. Ms. Patti chuckled, and Serena and Jill joined in.

"Enough about my craptastic day. What's going on with you two?" Serena flicked open the laminated menu, and began studying her choices.

"I bribed her into giving me her mother's chicken and dumplings recipe. Score!" Jill did a booty dance on her chair, fist bumping in the air. "She dug out the family recipe book and everything."

Ms. Patti glanced at Tessa. "Recipe book?"

"You should see it!" Jill grinned, nudging Tessa's arm. "It's so cool. All her relatives have recorded stuff in there. It goes back like—forever."

Tessa shook her head, barely suppressing her grin at Jill's exaggeration. "Not quite that long, though it has been in the family for a few generations. Recipes handed down from mother to daughter, and when my mom passed, the book came to me. It's one of the things I cherish, because of the memories it holds."

"How lovely." Serena's eyes met Tessa's for a split second, their expression haunted. Though they'd started building a tenuous friendship, Tessa didn't know a lot about Serena's background, or what her life had been like before moving to Shiloh Springs. Thinking back, she realized Serena rarely talked about her personal life. She'd have to make an extra effort to befriend the realtor who'd been nothing but kind to her since the moment they'd met.

"Would you allow me to look at it sometime?" Ms. Patti reached over and squeezed Serena's hand, though her words were directed at Tessa, and Tessa's gut told her the older woman was trying to steer the focus away from Serena's mention of her family. There was definitely something there, just beneath the surface. While she wouldn't pry, she wanted Serena to know she was there if she ever needed a friendly ear or a shoulder to cry on.

"Of course, anytime you'd like, Ms. Patti. There are lots of good, old fashioned Southern comfort recipes in there."

"Like her mother's chicken and dumplings. I swear, Tessa, your mom's dumplings were so light and airy, they practically floated out of the pot."

"Well, then, I definitely need that recipe, because it's one of Douglas' favorite meals."

Jill glanced toward the door, before smoothing her napkin across her lap, an amused expression flitting across her face. "Ladies, I think we've got company."

Looking up, Tessa immediately spotted Rafe, and a sizzle of heat flickered deep in her belly. He'd changed out of his uniform, now sporting a pair of dark jeans and a black T-shirt. Muscles bunched beneath the soft cotton, and she swallowed past her suddenly dry throat. Brody, Lucas, and Dane Boudreau stood with him, filling the doorway with an overload of testosterone. Every female head in the room turned, staring at the display of masculinity invading Daisy's place.

Waving a hand in front of her face, she leaned toward Ms. Patti. "I gotta say, you did raise some mighty fine-looking boys."

She chuckled. "You should have been around when they went through their terrible teen years. And their high school dating years…" She gave an exaggerated shudder.

Daisy waved a hand in their direction, pointing toward their table, and Rafe's gaze met hers. A slow, sexy smile curved his lips as he started toward her, and she swore she felt the room sway with his every step. His brothers trailed behind, but she barely noticed, her eyes glued to the man who occupied her every waking moment, and pretty much had since she'd met him.

"Well, if it isn't all my favorite ladies together in one place." The deep timbre of his voice seemed to reverberate deep inside her, sending a delighted shiver along her skin. He leaned in and kissed Ms. Patti's cheek, though his gaze never left hers. If she wasn't mistaken, the mischievous twinkle in their depths had her wanting to fan herself.

"Rafe…boys." Ms. Patti's voice held a teasing note, and she winked at Tessa before asking, "Would you like to join us?"

He grinned. "Thought you'd never ask."

"What are you doing in town? I thought you were headed to the Big House. Douglas put a big pot of chili on this afternoon, and I left a pan of cornbread in the oven."

"We're heading that way in a couple minutes, Momma. Dane spotted your car outside, and we thought we'd stop in long enough to say hello." Rafe's perusal had Tessa fidgeting in her chair, and she picked up the menu, fanning it in front of her face. "Though, if we'd know you had such lovely company, we'd have canceled plans with Dad and joined y'all for supper instead."

"Sorry, fellas, it's strictly ladies' night," Serena quipped.

"You sure? We'll even pay for dinner." Rafe winked and Tessa felt heat rush into her cheeks.

"Go on, your dad's waiting at the Big House." Ms. Patti pointed to her cheek, and each one dutifully pressed a kiss there. She gave them an indulgent smile. "I might have left a German chocolate cake for dessert."

"Well, why didn't you say so? See ya!" Lucas gave a mock bow. "Ladies."

After a bit more good-natured ribbing, the men headed for the diner's door. Jill sighed. "They look as good going as they do coming." At their burst of laughter, she slammed her hand against her mouth. "Did I say that out loud?"

Tessa nodded and Serena raised her hand to high five Jill. "You did, and I totally agree."

"Ladies, those are my sons you're ogling." Ms. Patti tried to look offended, but she couldn't pull it off, not with the look of pride as she watched her sons depart.

"Well, you gotta admit, you raised some mighty fine-looking sons." Serena raised her water glass. Tessa couldn't agree more.

"Enough about my brood. What's going on with you?" Ms. Patti's question enveloped the whole table, her steely-eyed gaze leaving nobody unscathed. "Come on, don't be shy. I've been at the ranch pretty much all week. Heath hadn't been back forty-eight hours before one of the mares caught him and busted his arm. I've been babying him like crazy, but I had to get out of the house before I drowned in testosterone. Luckily, Serena rescued me with a dinner invitation."

"Heath? Have I met him?" Tessa tried picturing all the Boudreau men, but couldn't place Heath.

"You probably met him at the barbecue. He's home for a visit. He lives in Virginia. Works in Washington for the ATF." Ms. Patti's tone was wistful. "Don't tell him I said this, but I really miss him. I'd give anything for him to move back home, but he seems happy living on the east coast."

"I don't remember him, but there were a lot of new faces that day."

"He was only here for a couple days and had to fly back for work. Then he showed up here earlier this week. I didn't have a clue he was coming, but I'm always glad when my boys show up. Although I wish he hadn't gotten hurt."

"Well, I don't have anything new going on in my life." Jill lifted her glass of water and took a sip. "I still hate my job. Hate my commute, but it pays the bills. And it keeps me out of trouble." Her cheeky grin was infectious and Tessa found herself smiling.

"Something better will come along, I promise. Look at me. I never expected to be in the same town with you, much less be working here. You never know, something new and exciting might be just around the corner, and you'll be happier than you've ever been."

"Well, I hope so. But can you speed up your timetable, because I'm not getting any younger."

"I agree with Tessa. New and exciting things happen all the time. I know it's hard, but be patient, and be open to new possibilities." Ms. Patti grabbed Jill's hand and squeezed it. "Did I ever say thank you for the beautiful cake you sent for the party?"

A blush spread across Jill's cheeks. "Yes, and thanks. I loved being able to contribute."

"I wish you'd have come. We missed you."

"Maybe next time." Tessa wasn't sure why her friend had decided not to come to the huge celebration, but she had a sneaking suspicion it had something to do with one of the brothers who'd been there in the diner. Whenever Lucas Boudreau's name was mentioned, Jill got quiet and withdrawn. Tessa wasn't above prying if need be, to find out what was troubling her friend, and try to fix whatever the problem was. Because that's what friends do, they help.

Their food arrived, and disappeared as quickly as it came. Before long, it was time to call it a night. Giving each woman a hug, she climbed behind the wheel, and started the engine. With a soft sigh and a shrug, she decided she'd wait and go to the grocery store in the morning. She didn't feel like heading back to the school to grab the recipe book. It was safe enough there overnight, locked in her desk.

Turning up the radio, she sang with the music all the way home. Tonight had been fun, and she hoped they'd get together again soon. She hoped Rafe and his brothers had fun with Douglas. She was looking forward to supper tomorrow night, and planned on making one of her grandmother's recipes.

With a smile, she climbed the steps and headed inside.

She couldn't wait for tomorrow.

CHAPTER TWENTY

"Evan, what are you doing here? Is Beth with you?"

"Guess it is a surprise, seeing me." He gave her a sheepish grin, eyes downcast. "I had a business meeting in Austin, and thought I'd drive out and see my favorite sister-in-law before heading home. Beth would bite my head off, knowing I was this close and didn't at least drop by and make sure you're doing okay."

Tessa stepped back and held the door open wider. "Come in. Sorry, I'm surprised to see you. How are Beth and Jamie? I miss them so much."

Closing the door behind him, she couldn't help noticing he looked a bit haggard, something totally out of character for her normally meticulous brother-in-law. Evan took pride in his appearance. He defined the word metrosexual. Never a hair out of place, shirts always ironed with nary a single wrinkle. Pants pressed with the perfect crease. Today, his hair appeared windswept and messy, like he'd slept on it wrong and it hadn't seen a comb since. If she didn't know better, she'd think he'd slept in his clothes too.

"They're good, though Jamie misses her Aunt Tessa."

She watched him look around the living room, taking it in. "Nice place."

"Thanks. I like it."

"Tessa…" He stopped, letting her name trail off to a bare whisper. Shaking his head, he took a step forward, until he stood close. *Too close.* "Everything's gone to hell, and I'm out of options."

She eased back, but froze when his hand latched onto her wrist, his fingers tight as a steel manacle, and she winced in pain. Staring into his face, she recoiled at the undisguised anger and hatred burning in his eyes. His lips twisted into an ugly grimace. She'd never been afraid of Evan before, but now he scared her.

"Let me go!"

"I can't. Not until you tell me what you did with it."

"What I did with what? Evan, you're not making any sense." She pushed at his chest with her free hand, trying to break free of his iron hold. "I don't have anything of yours."

"Yeah, you do." She cringed at the frantic note in his words, the panicked expression on his face, even while his eyes desperately scanned her living room. He was searching for something. "I've hunted high and low. Checked every square inch of your parents' house. I've gone through everything Beth saved, and it's not there. You have to have it!"

He wasn't making sense, and he sounded crazy. Like he was at the end of his rope and hanging by a thread. From his words, it obvious he was looking for something, but she didn't have a clue. From his actions—well, those spoke volumes, if his death grip on her arm was any indication.

"Maybe I'm being dense, but I don't know what you mean. If you tell me, I'll help, but you have to let me go first." Tessa did her best to keep her voice soft and calm. The grip on her wrist didn't loosen. If anything, it felt even tighter. The knot in the pit of her stomach tightened, and her breath caught in her chest. He was scaring her.

"The bond. Don't act so surprised. I know you have it. Think you can cheat me out of my share? Give it to me now!"

Bond? What bond?

"Don't act stupid, Tessa. The Crowley County bond. The one your great-grandfather bought before the turn of the century."

Wait—he wants a useless piece of paper? It's not worth anything. It's nothing more than a piece of family heritage.

"Wait a second. When did you go through my parents' house?" The lead ball feeling in the middle of her stomach grew. Dear heavens, please let her be wrong. Because if the direction her thoughts were taking proved correct...

"I looked everywhere. Searched their place from basement to attic. Heck, I almost thought I imagined the damned thing." The intensity in his burning gaze locked her in place, and her feet froze to the floor. "You've seen it. I know Beth has, because we talked about it a couple of times.

I remembered your family talking about it, so I started digging."

"Evan, I swear I don't have it. If Beth doesn't, it's long gone, probably donated with the stuff we gave to charity."

"Liar!"

With a hard shove, he pushed her away. She tumbled to the floor, her elbow smacking against the hardwood surface when she landed. Instantaneous pain flared through her arm, followed by a throbbing ache. She scooted away from him, cradling her arm against her chest. Her only thought—get as far away from Evan as she could. Something must have set him off, because this wasn't the Evan she knew. He'd never acted like this before. When had he become obsessed with a worthless piece of paper?

"Evan—"

"You'd better pray it's here, Tessa. Otherwise…"

"What?"

Do I really want to know the answer?

His smile resembled a twisted, macabre mask as he ran a hand through his blond hair, making it wilder than before. But what scared her even more was the gun in his hand. The hand which moments earlier he'd clamped around her wrist. She couldn't take her eyes off the dull matte finish of the metal, or the way Evan's hand didn't shake. It was rock steady, the barrel pointed straight at her head. If he fired, there'd be no dodging that bullet.

"You always make things difficult, don't you, Tessa?

Moved halfway across the country. Forced me to chase you. I know the bond wasn't in the stuff you left behind. I went through it. Why'd you need all this stupid crap anyway?"

"Jamie never went through the boxes, did she? It was you." Tessa remembered calling when the boxes arrived, and Evan's tall tale about Jamie opening them while he was on a phone call. It had been a lie—everything had been a lie.

"I followed you here. Tossed this place, and still couldn't find it. Of course, it's easy to hide a single sheet of paper. Where is the bond, Tessa? I'm not going back empty handed this time."

"You're the one who trashed my house? Destroyed the furniture and—"

"Yeah, yeah. It was me. I'm the villain. Boo hoo." He loomed over her, and the maniacal gleam in his eyes told her everything she needed to know about his intensions and his mental state. Once he got his hands on the Crowley County bond, her usefulness was at an end. He couldn't afford to let her live, because he knew she wouldn't hesitate an instant before turning him in to the cops.

There was just one problem. She didn't have the bond.

Time slowed like molasses in Alaska as reality hit. He mentioned he'd been digging into info about the bond. Did it mean—could it mean—the bond wasn't worthless? The family never redeemed the bond. They'd held onto it, considered it their gift to the county as a family heirloom. The Maxwell's handed it down from generation to generation as a reminder of their family's support for their fledgling North Carolina community. Crowley County sold the municipal bonds at the turn of the century, raising money for different things including roadways, building schools, and the courthouse. Then she had another thought, one which chilled her to her marrow.

"The phone calls? Were you the one making the phone calls with the blocked number?"

He smirked. "Not me personally. I had help." His malicious chuckle sent chills racing down her spine. "It wasn't hard to convince Trevor you were playing hard to get, though he did mention how frightened you sounded. I think he got turned on by scaring you. He didn't mind throwing a bit of a scare into you, said you deserved it for running away from him. Believe it or not, he still wants to marry you."

"Where is he?"

"Closer than you think."

Which explained the eerie feeling she'd had for the last several days. Darn it, she should have trusted her instincts—and she should have told Rafe.

"He's here?" She breathed out the words, though she already knew the answer. She rubbed her hands along her arms, feeling the chill bumps along her skin.

"I couldn't keep flying to Texas, could I? Beth might get suspicious. I could write off the first trip as business. This one? I lied about having a business meeting. Right now, everyone thinks I'm in San Francisco."

She drew in a ragged breath when the gun lowered slightly, though it was only a moment's reprieve. Evan was smart. Brilliant, really. Apparently, he was also a stark-raving lunatic.

"Does Beth know you're looking for the bond?" *Please, please*, she prayed, *don't let her be involved in Evan's scheme.* She'd had enough pain in her life recently, she couldn't bear the thought of losing her sister too.

"Your sister is too stupid and too naïve. She'd never be able to keep from telling you everything. Besides," he lifted the gun again, the barrel pointed straight at her forehead, "I'm afraid, like you, she's going to suffer a tragic accident soon, conveniently leaving our daughter the sole beneficiary of her life insurance policy, as well as the Crowley County bond."

The breath caught in Tessa throat at his threat, followed by a burning hot rage deep in her gut that quickly spread upward like a roaring fire, engulfing her in its ferocity. "Why are you doing this?" She barely got the words out, her jaw tensed so tight it might shatter into a million pieces. Bracing against the coffee table, she levered up to a standing position. "Is this about money? I don't have much, just what I have from my share of my parents' life insurance, but I'll give it to you."

His eye roll made her want to punch him. "You're nearly as stupid as your sister. Do you realize how much an unclaimed county bond is worth? In today's market, that five-hundred-dollar piece of paper, with the interest compounded annually for over a hundred and twenty years, is worth millions. And I intend to cash it in, and live very happily."

Her eyes widened at his statement. Could it possibly be true? "I'm telling you the honest truth, Evan. I don't know where the Crowley County bond is—I haven't seen it in years. But," she held up a hand to stop him when he started to interrupt, "we can look for it together. I've unpacked everything I brought with me, and the boxes Beth shipped. Maybe it's here and I missed it somehow."

She prayed he'd agree. It might buy her some time to come up with a plan, because she was out of options. Terrified he'd shoot her. More afraid somebody would show up on her doorstep, and he'd hurt them. Living in a small town like Shiloh Springs, her house oftentimes resembled a revolving door. People were always stopping by, mostly Boudreaus. Her heart clenched at the thought of any of them stepping into the line of fire.

Especially Rafe.

"We can start in the office. I put most of the things in there." Holding her hands out to her sides, palms facing forward, she walked slowly toward the office door, which stood ajar. She heard Evan's footsteps behind her. There was no chance to get in and lock the door before he could stop her. And she couldn't forget, he had a gun.

"I looked here before." His gaze swept the room, which

had been put back to rights after the police had processed the scene. The rage burning in her chest intensified, sweeping upward like a fiery red tidal wave, its slow burn feeding her anger.

"So we check again." Kneeling beside the bookcase, she lifted several books free, and began shaking them upside down, and several papers fluttered to the floor. Notes from classes. Scribbled lists. She'd gotten into the habit of stuffing papers into her books, using them as bookmarks, or a way to keep them together. The way her mother had done for years.

Wait—like her mother? The answer was so simple.

Tessa knew where the bond was.

CHAPTER TWENTY-ONE

B rody turned off the ignition, and listened as his sister complained—again—about having to head back to school when she'd rather be home for the rest of summer. Was it his fault she'd signed up for extra classes? That's the price she paid for wanting to graduate early. He touched the Bluetooth, turning down the volume, because Nica was on a roll, and *her* volume increased the longer she rambled.

He'd spotted lights on at Tessa's place, and decided to make a quick stop, see how things were, and if she needed anything now school had started. The pretty little redhead had quickly worked her way into the hearts of all the Boudreaus, including his. She'd had the biggest impact on big brother Rafe, and Brody couldn't be happier. Rafe deserved some happiness, and Tessa seemed to care about his brother too.

When Tessa's front door opened and she stepped out, he spotted a blond man grasping her arm. She attempted to wrench it free without success. The look on her face was one he recognized instantly, because in his job with the fire department he saw it far too often not to recognize it.

Fear.

The stranger manhandled her toward a four-door sedan parked in the drive, and Brody took note of the rental sticker on its back window. Flipping open the glove compartment, he scrambled for something to write on, and jotted down the license plate number. He wasn't sure why, except his gut told him something wasn't right, and he'd learned a long time ago to follow his instincts.

The blond man shoved Tessa into the back seat, slid in beside her and slammed the door. A dark-haired man occupied the driver's seat, and was far enough away Brody couldn't get a good look at him. Within seconds, the car backed onto the street, and pulled away, Tessa's pale face illuminated by the streetlight.

"Brody, are you listening to me?"

He'd forgotten about his sister, too intent on watching Tessa and the stranger. "Nica, I've gotta go. Call you later."

"Wait—"

Cutting off the call, he dialed Rafe's number. Pulling onto the asphalt, he followed the other car. Maybe he was making too much of things, but the way the guy had manhandled Tessa didn't sit well. Especially knowing she'd been getting harassing calls and her place had been trashed. Better safe than sorry.

"Hello." His brother's voice sounded distracted and a bit grumpy.

"Can you run a license plate for me?"

"What? Why?"

Brody drew in a deep breath, praying Rafe would keep his cool after he heard why Brody was calling. "I was on my way to your place. We're supposed to watch the game tonight, remember?"

"And?"

"I saw Tessa's lights on. Thought I'd stop in and see if she needed anything. When I got here, there was a strange car in her driveway. Then she came out with some guy, who had a pretty wicked-looking grip on her arm."

A string of curses blasted through the earpiece, and he cringed at the volume and tone in his brother's voice.

"Where are you now?"

"Following their car." Brody watched the taillights, staying several car lengths behind. He knew every road, trail, and bike path in the entire town, and wasn't about to lose them. Whoever was behind the wheel didn't do anything to draw attention to the sedan, right down to using turn signals. His brow furrowed when they turned into the elementary school parking lot. Through the Bluetooth, he heard a door slam, knew Rafe was headed for his own car, ready to give chase.

"Bro, they're at the elementary school."

"Stay back until I get there and can assess the situation. Have they spotted you?"

"Don't think so." Flicking off his headlights, he parked on a side street, afraid if he pulled into the parking lot, it would be a dead giveaway they'd been followed. "They got out of the car, and Tessa is motioning toward the door."

"I'll be there in three minutes." The silence following Rafe's statement was eloquent, and Brody heard his brother draw in a ragged breath. "If you think she's in trouble—"

"I'll keep your girl safe, bro. Just get here."

The strangers and Tessa headed toward the school. Tessa dug something out of her jeans' pocket and handed it to the blond man, who unlocked the door. As soon as they entered, Brody raced across the blacktopped parking lot. Following his instincts, he cut around the side of the building, headed for the windows of Tessa's classroom. Some sixth sense told him where they were headed, because he couldn't think of any other reason for coming to the elementary school.

The overhead lights in her classroom flashed on, and he crouched low, staying in the shadows. From this angle, he got a pretty good view of the room, as well as the two men. The dark-haired one's smirk grated on Brody's nerves. There was a cruel set to his mouth, and his eyes never left Tessa.

Tessa jerked her arm free from the blond man's grip, rubbing at her elbow. Her glare didn't show fear, though she did take a couple of steps away from him. The blond said something he couldn't hear through the closed classroom windows. He really wanted, no, needed to hear what was going on. Studying the aluminum casing, he noted they were the older kind with the swivel crank, and they opened outward.

He slid his fingers under the metal groove, pulling toward him, and mentally crossed his fingers the window didn't squeak or make any sound. It stuck, refusing to budge. Bracing a shoulder against the wall, he tugged harder, finally feeling it move. He knew he couldn't open it far, maybe an inch or so—enough to hear what was happening.

"I'm here."

Brody congratulated himself on not screaming like a little girl when Rafe spoke, though it had been a close call. Dang, his brother moved quietly when he needed to. He squatted next to Brody, his eyes glued on Tessa.

Brody jerked his head toward the window, a finger to his lips. Rafe leaned in closer, his gaze frozen to the tableau unfolding inside the classroom. From the tightness of his body, Brody knew his brother was close to losing it. Totally unlike his usually unflappable big brother. It served to reinforce how much Rafe cared for Tessa.

"You said you knew where the bond is, Tessa."

"Evan, please, I'll give it to you, but not until I know Beth and Jamie are okay."

"Evan?" Brody mouthed the name.

Rafe whispered, "Her brother-in-law."

"Do you know the other dude?" Brody kept his voice to a whisper. Rafe shook his head, his face blank, but Brody knew his brother. If either of those men harmed Tessa, there'd be no stopping him. No second chances. Not even his badge would spare them.

"This is ridiculous." The darker-haired stranger started

knocking books off the shelf beside him, sending them tumbling to the ground. "I'm tired of messing around. Get the damned bond, Tessa."

Rafe scooted closer to Brody, his eyes glued to the three people in the classroom. "Think you can break the window and get inside when I signal you?" At his nod, Rafe continued, "I'm going to circle around and go inside. You hold the fort here until I'm in position. I'll handle these two jerks. Your job is to keep Tessa safe, got it?"

"Bro, I've got my shotgun in my truck. I'm going to run and grab it, just in case. I'll be back in position before you make it down the hall." Rafe nodded and squeezed Brody's shoulder.

"Be careful. We don't know if they're armed."

"You, too." Rafe disappeared into the shadows, and Brody raced to his truck and grabbed the shotgun he kept behind the seat. Growing up on a ranch in Texas, he didn't know anybody who didn't own and carry guns. Too many critters, both four and two-legged, kept a man on his toes. Snagging the gun and a handful of shells, he jogged back and got into position by Tessa's classroom window once again.

He eased his hand between the aluminum casing of the window and the window's frame, tugged it open another inch or two, stopping only when it gave a squeak of protest. Checking to assure the shotgun was loaded, he slid the barrel through the small opening, his stare zeroed in on the people inside the classroom. The twenty-two probably wouldn't kill either man, but they'd be in a world of hurt, and it would give Rafe the break he needed to get Tessa outta there.

Tessa and both men stood near the front, between her desk and the blackboard. The classroom door was ajar, enough he'd be able to see Rafe when he got into position.

Now, all he could do was wait—and pray they escaped unscathed—because if anything happened to Tessa, he wasn't sure his big brother would survive it.

CHAPTER TWENTY-TWO

Tessa watched Evan's face turn a mottled shade of red. If he didn't calm down, he was headed for a stroke or a coronary. Not that she'd cry about it—not after his threats to hurt Beth and precious Jamie. He could rot in purgatory, as far as she was concerned. Of course, Trevor's continual egging him on didn't help matters. When had these two become so buddy-buddy? The entire time she'd dated Trevor, he'd acted like he couldn't stand Evan, going so far as to cancel whenever she made plans for them to spend time with Beth and her husband. Yet here they stood, apparently working together to steal something belonging to her family.

I need to stall, figure out how to get away from these lunatics. I can't give them what they want, or tomorrow morning I'll be the headline of the local news, early edition. Teacher's body found in classroom. Film at eleven.

"Tessa." Trevor took a step closer. The maniacal gleam in his eyes sent a jolt of fear ricocheting through her. Her heartbeat thumped in her chest, faster and faster, until she thought it might explode. Another step backward, and her legs bumped against her desk. She hadn't realized she'd taken a step for every one he'd taken toward her. Like a cornered animal, she fought the urge to lash out. From the feral look in his eyes, he'd retaliate. "Don't be like this, baby. Give Evan what he wants, then you and I can walk away—be together like we're meant to be."

Has he lost his mind?

"Why should I?"

Evan stood silent, his gazed fixated on her, without a single emotion present on his face. He reminded her of a snake who'd cornered his prey, toying with it, waiting for the perfect opportunity to strike the killing bite. She'd never been afraid of him before. Then again, he had never given her a reason to fear him. Now? His façade of civility disappeared, peeled away layer-by-layer, and true evil shone in his eyes. A shiver skittered down her spine and chill bumps spread across her skin.

"Stop wasting time, Tessa." Evan's voice echoed in the empty classroom, cold and hollow, the words filled with an almost tangible menace. "You said you'd take me—us—to the bond. We're here." His hand whipped out and gripped her throat, faster than she could move. As his fingers tightened, the breath caught in her chest, and she struggled for each breath. Little black dots appeared before her eyes, and she wondered if her next breath would be her last.

With a sound of disgust, Evan pushed her away, and Tessa gasped for air, her hand touching her throat. Time was up. She couldn't stall any longer. But she wasn't ready to die.

There was too much to live for, so much she wanted to experience. Her life had changed since moving to Shiloh Springs, in the best way possible. It couldn't end now, not before she had a chance to tell Rafe she'd fallen in love with him.

"Ms. Maxwell, is everything okay here? I saw the lights on and thought I'd stop by and check."

Rafe! Rafe was here.

"Everything's fine, Sheriff Boudreau." She emphasized his title, following his lead. Evan's almost imperceptible flinch when she mentioned his name was quickly hidden when he took a step toward Rafe, his hand outstretched.

"Sheriff, I'm Evan Stewart, Tessa's brother-in-law. It's nice to meet you. My associate and I are in Texas on a business trip. Tessa's sister, my wife, would have my head if I didn't stop and check on her."

"That's right," Trevor added, coming to stand next to Tessa and he grabbed her hand, interlocking their fingers. He gripped it hard enough she almost let out a yelp, biting her lip to keep from making a sound. "Tessa and I have a long history together. I couldn't let my best girl miss me too much." He brushed a kiss against her cheek, and nausea writhed in her belly, threatening to make its way out. She squeezed her eyes shut, fighting the urge to upchuck all over his shiny shoes. "I'm trying to convince her how much I've missed her."

Rafe's eyes swept over each of them, and Tessa silently

prayed he'd figure out she was in trouble. Even if he did, she couldn't see a way out of this without violence. She'd never seen Evan like this, acting like he had nothing to lose.

"I, um, thought I'd show them my classroom, since I spend so much of my time here. Evan can tell my sister about my life here, how I'm not fitting in, and how much I want to come home." *Please, Rafe, get the message. You know I love it in Shiloh Springs. I'm happy for the first time in a long time, and I don't want Evan or Trevor to ruin everything.*

"I understand. I know things haven't worked out the way you'd planned." Rafe turned his attention to Evan. "If you wouldn't mind, I'd like to speak with Ms. Maxwell for a moment—in private. We'll be right over there. It'll only take a second." He pointed toward the back of the classroom. Evan looked back and forth between the two, his mouth set in a mulish frown, before he finally nodded.

Tessa jerked her hand free from Trevor's and wiped it along her thigh. His every touch made her skin crawl, and she'd need a gallon of bleach to get rid of the sensation of him touching her.

"Rafe, I need to tell you something." She kept her voice low, barely a whisper, but she knew he heard her.

"I know. Brody saw them hustle you out of your place and into their car. I'm stalling long enough for him to get in place before I make a move. Are you alright? Did they hurt you?"

She shook her head, wrapping her arms across her chest.

Every nerve in her body felt like it was on high alert, wound tight as a spring ready to pop. "I'm fine, just scared. Evan has a gun. I'm not sure about Trevor, but he probably does, too."

"Everything's going to be okay, I promise. Any idea why they're here, why they'd risk kidnapping you? Seems pretty risky, taking a chance of somebody seeing them. It was pure luck Brody happened to spot them when he did."

"It's a long story, but I have something they want. Evan thinks it's worth a lot of money. I can't let him get his hands on it." She lowered her voice to a bare whisper, and he leaned in, close enough she could smell the masculine scent that was his alone. "Rafe, I think he's insane. He threatened to kill Beth," she didn't add the threat to her own life, "and take Jamie."

"You almost finished, Tessa? We've still got a lot to talk about." Evan walked closer, and Tessa's hands started shaking. Rafe had said Brody was here somewhere. Where was he? Time was running out, and Evan's patience with it.

Rafe gently took her elbow and led her back to the front of the classroom. "I think we've covered everything. Tessa, I'll speak with Mr. Sanchez, and see if we can get you out of your contract. Shiloh Springs will find another teacher to take over. No one wants you to be unhappy. If going back to North Carolina is the answer, I promise I'll make it happen."

"That's great, Sheriff—Boudreau, was it?" Trevor grinned like he'd been given the biggest Christmas present under the tree. "You've made me very happy, letting my gal come back home. Where she belongs."

"Thank you, Sheriff Boudreau. I can't wait to leave Shiloh Springs. Being away from my family, it's been tougher than I expected. Leaving the kids will be hard, but they'll adjust. They're young and adaptable. It'll be fine." Tessa hated lying. She loved the kids in her class. They'd built a rapport and trusted her, participating in the classroom, excited about the new books and stories Tessa had introduced. Some of the kids had started bringing her little treats to brighten her week. She'd never leave them, not like this.

"Hey, bro, everything cool?" Brody's voice came through loud and clear from the open window. Evan and Trevor spun toward the new threat, and Rafe reached forward, pulling Tessa behind him, whipping his gun from the back of his waistband.

"Yeah, I've got it covered."

Evan spun around and spotted the gun in Rafe's hand, and froze, hand halfway toward his own gun. Rafe shook his head slowly, and motioned for him to put his hands up. Trevor's gaze darted between Evan and Rafe, before looking at Tessa with a hate-filled glare.

"This is your fault!" Trevor's bellow of rage echoed off the walls of the classroom. "You ruined everything." With an unintelligible roar, he rushed toward Tessa. The sound of a gunshot reverberated loudly, and Trevor fell to the ground, clutching his thigh. Blood pooled beneath his fingers, and he started wailing, screaming for a doctor.

"Tessa, tell the sheriff this has all been a misunderstanding. Nobody needs to get hurt."

"You're right, nobody else needs to get hurt, if you keep your hands where I can see them." Rafe glanced to the window. "You okay, bro?"

"Better than the fellow on the floor. I already called this in and backup should be here any minute."

"Thanks, Brody."

Tessa collapsed against the doorframe, her whole body trembling from the adrenaline rocketing through her bloodstream. Trevor's screams had faded down to pitiful cries, accompanied by him rocking back and forth. Blood pooled onto the floor beneath his thigh, and he blubbered like a three-year-old with a boo-boo. Evan's eyes darted between her and Rafe, dead and lifeless like a shark studying its prey. She prayed he didn't do anything stupid. Before tonight, she'd never have thought him capable of violence. Now, she wouldn't put anything past him. Underestimating him would be a mistake.

"My brother's still at the window, with a shotgun pointed at you, Stewart." Rafe held the pistol in his hand in a steady grip. "You've heard what they say about Texans, haven't you? We tend to shoot first and ask questions later. Sometimes we don't even bother with the questions. I'd suggest you don't try anything stupid. Turn around slowly and put your hands on top of your head." With a muttered curse, Evan complied. Rafe walked forward slowly until he stood right behind him. Reaching forward, he pulled the gun from Evan's waistband and tucked it into his own. "Get down on your knees, and keep your hands atop your head."

Within seconds, Rafe had cuffs on Evan, and sat him against the wall. Trevor rocked slowly, cradling his thigh, tears streaking his face. Tessa heard sirens in the distance, and her body slumped with relief. It was over. Beth was safe. Little Jamie was safe. She gave a watery smile at Brody, who stood outside the classroom, his rifle still pointed at the two men who'd caused so much trouble.

"Are you okay?" Rafe watched her, studying her face intently. With her shaky nod, he pulled her into his arms, holding her close. His hand cradled the back of her head. She felt him draw in a ragged breath, and wrapped her arms around him, resting her forehead against his.

"I can't believe you saved me."

"I will always save you, sweetheart. I gotta admit though, I hope I don't have to ride to the rescue too often. I'm getting too old for this." His teasing grin drew an answering smile from Tessa.

"You know I didn't mean anything I said back there? I love it here. Shiloh Springs, the kids." She desperately wanted to add his name to the list of the things she loved, but didn't. She was afraid. A coward. Her feelings were too new, too raw. Soon, she'd tell him soon, but for now being held in his arms, knowing the danger was over had to be enough.

First responders poured through the open classroom door. They immediately went to Trevor, and went to work on his gunshot wound. Dusty yanked Evan to his feet none-too-gently, and escorted him from the room, reciting his Miranda rights as they walked away.

"I'm going to have to go to the sheriff's department and get these two booked. You'll have to make a statement. Are you up for that, sweetheart? It can wait until morning, if you need time."

"It's okay, let's get this over with." She closed her eyes and drew in a shuddering breath. "I'm wondering what to tell Beth. This is going to destroy her."

"Let's wait for the smoke to clear, and we'll call her together. Okay?"

"Sure. I can't believe Evan did all this for a lousy bond."

Rafe leaned back and looked at her. "That's right, you haven't told me what they wanted."

"Evan and Trevor came looking for a county bond. It's been in my family for generations. A part of my family history. Nobody really thought much of it, but it's a county bond purchased over a hundred years ago for five hundred dollars. My family wanted to help Crowley County grow; we were doing our part. Evan heard about the bond and did a little digging into the county records. Found out it's worth a couple million."

"Dollars?"

"Uh-huh. I hate to say this, but—I think Evan might have had something to do with my parents' deaths." Her words came out a croaked whisper. "I think he's insane."

"I'll get in touch with the authorities, give them the information on what's happened here, and maybe they'll look a little deeper into what happened. Now, let's get the paperwork done, so we can go home."

Home. Such a simple word, but so profound. She'd found her home, here in Shiloh Springs, but more importantly in Rafe's arms. Was it too much to hope he felt the same?

CHAPTER TWENTY-THREE

"What's going to happen to them—Evan and Trevor?" Rafe pulled her closer against his side, still reeling from the aftershocks and adrenaline rush from everything at the elementary school. After leaving the sheriff's station, he'd driven them back to his place. Even with Evan Stewart and Trevor St. James behind bars, he didn't want Tessa out of his sight, not for a second. He couldn't forget the terror of almost losing her.

He smoothed a hand over her hair in a soothing motion. "They'll both stand trial for multiple counts of attempted murder, including special circumstances of using a firearm, as well as kidnapping. If they're smart, they'll try to make a deal with the prosecutor. Texans don't play around when it comes to cases like this. Chances are good they'll spend the rest of their lives behind bars."

"I can't believe Evan did this." She bolted upright beside him, a panicked look crossing her face. "What am I going to tell Beth?"

The sight of tears welling in her beautiful blue eyes nearly broke him. How could he not sympathize? Growing up with a dysfunctional and ugly beginning got turned around because of Douglas and Patti Boudreau. Life had taught him one valuable lesson. Family meant everything. Hugging her tighter, he rested his chin on top her head, and felt the slight tremble in her body. "You tell her you love her. That none of Evan's actions are her fault. And you'll be there for her and Jamie, because they're going to need you, probably more than they yet realize."

"It's all so senseless. We never realized the bond was worth anything. My mom called it a reminder of our heritage, the Maxwell family helping establish Crowley County. To us, it was simply a piece of history, a show of our family's support for the county they loved. I can't wrap my head around a simple piece of paper being worth so much money." She blew out a breath, the puff of air rustling a tendril of hair that drifted across her forehead, and he reached up, gently brushing it back.

"People do crazy things for money, sweetheart. I guess what they say is true—the love of money is the root of all evil." Leaning back, he propped his feet atop the coffee table, his muscles finally starting to relax. It felt right, having Tessa wrapped in his embrace, her body curled against his, head snuggled against his shoulder. It was a feeling he wanted to relive every single day for the rest of his life.

"I have to go back. To North Carolina."

Tension rolled through him, muscles bunching beneath his skin. Here it was. The inevitable, horrible black moment he'd been dreading since getting the phone call from Brody about Tessa being in danger.

"I understand." Though he spoke the words, deep in his gut, every dream he'd built about the two of them together wilted and crumbled to dust. He'd let her go back to North Carolina, be with her sister and her niece, but inside, he died a little.

Like hell I will. I love her. I'm not giving up on her—on us.

He'd spent the last several weeks getting to know her, seen the way she fit seamlessly into his life and into his heart. If she thought she could walk away without him fighting for her, for them, she had another think coming.

"I have to call Mr. Sanchez. Let him know what's happened. I need to be with Beth—she'll need me. Beth and Jamie have so much to process. I need to be there, to help her through the shock." Her eyes glistened with unshed tears, and he wrapped his arm around her, squeezing her tight.

"Tessa," her name caught in his throat.

She continued as though he hadn't spoken. "I know I haven't been here long, but under the circumstances, I think he'll give me a few weeks off, don't you?"

A few weeks off?

"You're coming back?"

"Of course. I love Shiloh Springs." Her eyes widened. "You thought I wasn't going to come back?"

He couldn't answer, emotion clogging his throat. He

simply nodded.

Gentle hands cupped his face, and he stared into the most beautiful sapphire eyes he'd ever seen. Her thumb swept softly against his cheek, and he heard the soft rasp of his five o'clock shadow beneath her gentle touch. "Rafe, I'm not leaving permanently. I want to stay—with you. Things have been crazy since I got here. It feels like I've been on a roller coaster from the minute I hit town." She grinned, her eyes alight with mischief. "Have I mentioned I love roller coasters?"

"Not that I recall."

"Meeting you, getting to know the man behind the badge, opened my eyes to a whole new life. You are a kind, generous, sometimes bossy, but totally lovable man, and I've fallen head-over-heels in love with you."

"Tessa, sweetheart—"

"I'm still talking." She gave him a cheeky grin, and he melted inside. "I didn't plan on falling in love. All I wanted was a little time away from everything. The grief, the confusion, everything back in North Carolina. Instead, I got threatened with being tossed in jail the minute I arrived in Shiloh Springs. Then your family swept me up in their tidal wave of craziness and love, and I knew I'd finally found the place I belonged. Finding you, loving you, was a bonus I never expected, but I wouldn't change anything. Not one second, because it led me to the love I've searched for my whole life. You, Rafe Boudreau, are my dream come true."

"Can I talk now?" He felt like the grin on his face couldn't get any bigger, and the love welling inside his chest couldn't be contained any longer.

"I guess so." She gave him the cutest wink and settled against his side, her head on his shoulder once again. Which felt right. It felt perfect, like she belonged there. How had he ever lived without her?

"The first day I met you, I was dumbstruck. Even before I saw your face, there was a connection, like Fate had slapped me upside the head, because I'd never felt anything like it before."

"The first time you saw me, you were looking at my butt."

"And it is a truly spectacular butt, darlin'." Her body shook with laughter, and he pulled her closer.

"Thank you, kind sir."

"I admit I was fascinated by the redhead on Old Man Johnson's front porch, but it was more than that. I couldn't stop thinking about you. I made up excuses to show up at places where I knew you'd be, so I'd have a reason to talk to you. When things started snowballing out of control, and you started getting threats, I nearly lost it. You have no idea how hard it was not bringing you here, locking you away so nobody could hurt you. That's when I knew I was gone. Round-the-bend, over-the-moon, totally and forever in love with you.

"Rafe—"

"You got to talk, now I get to have my say. I think I loved you from the first and it's only gotten stronger, more intense, until all I want is to be with you every minute of every day. To see you smile. To hear you laugh. To kiss you breathless. I'm not an idiot. I know we're moving fast, but I've never been surer of anything in my life. I love you, Tessa Maxwell."

"I love you, Rafe Boudreau."

Rafe leaned in, brushing his lips against hers, the sweetest kiss he'd ever had, reverent and worshipful. He pulled back, staring into her eyes, and read the love shining within them. He started to delve back in for another taste, but an insistent pounding on the front door broke them apart.

"Ignore them, maybe they'll go away."

Tessa giggled. "You really think so?"

The banging continued, growing louder, and Ms. Patti's voice could be heard through the door. "Rafe Boudreau, I know you're in there. You open this door right now."

Rafe's head fell forward into his hands. "She's not going away."

"Open the door, son." Douglas' voice joined his wife's.

"They really won't leave until we answer."

Rafe opened the front door, and braced himself as his momma barreled inside, throwing herself against him and wrapping her arms around him. He almost staggered at her momentum, and then caught her up in a bear hug.

"Where's Tessa? Is she alright?"

"I'm fine, Ms. Patti," Tessa smiled as she moved to stand beside Rafe. Completely ignoring him now, Rafe watched his mother pull Tessa into a hug. His dad stood at his side and watched the two women exchange soft words, Ms. Patti holding Tessa like she was her long-lost child.

"I heard there was a bit of trouble tonight." Douglas watched his son with compassion and a bit of amusement.

"You might say that. Brother-in-law thought Tessa had something he wanted."

"Ah. Explains a lot. Brody said there was a bit of a tussle, but y'all ended it without too much trouble."

"Brody got to have all the fun. He shot one of 'em."

Douglas laughed and slapped him on the back. "He might have neglected to mention that little fact." He gestured toward Tessa. "You gonna let her get away?"

Rafe couldn't hide his grin. "Nope. Though you did interrupt me telling her I love her."

Douglas studied him before a huge grin split his face. "Congratulations, son. You picked a good one. May you be as happy with Tessa as I am with your momma."

"Thanks, Dad."

"What happens now?"

"Evan and Trevor, the two idiots from tonight, are probably going away for a long time. Tessa needs to head to North Carolina for a bit, explain things to her sister. I'm thinking about going with her, if I can get the sheriff's department covered."

"Don't worry about it, son. We've all got your back. I'll talk to the mayor."

His father marched across the living room and lifted Tessa into a hug, while his mother looked on proudly. Knowing his family approved helped, but he'd have stuck with Tessa no matter what. She was his world now, his everything.

When she turned in his direction and smiled, he knew everything would be okay. No, better than okay. His life was perfect.

CHAPTER TWENTY-FOUR
EPILOGUE

Antonio Boudreau parked in front of the Big House and cut the engine. The tension he'd carried all the way from Dallas eased as he stared at the place he'd called home for most of his teenage years. A sense of peace pervaded, settling around him like a warm blanket. *Home.* There wasn't another place on earth he'd found that made him feel the way returning to the Big House did, like the final piece of a jigsaw puzzle snapping into place.

He'd gotten a call from his father, and immediately took a few days off and drove straight through. Douglas wouldn't have called if it wasn't important, so he'd dropped everything and headed to Shiloh Springs. When he'd mentioned Rafe being in trouble and needing help, he hadn't questioned it, because there was no question needed. Family came first—always.

"You going to sit here all night, or are you coming in?" Brody stood outside his open car window, grinning. His brother looked lean and fit, not surprising since he worked at Shiloh Springs Fire Station. The demands of the job kept him in shape, and when he wasn't fighting fires, he worked around the ranch, helping Dane keep things running smooth. All of the Boudreaus pitched in whenever they had the chance.

"I just got here. I was looking at the place. Every time I pull up the drive, it's like coming home."

"That's because it is home, jackass." Brody pulled open the door, and Antonio slid out and stretched, feeling the pull in his muscles after the long drive.

"Not what I meant, bro. It's more than the place we grew up. There's a sense of rightness here, a feeling of belonging. I miss it."

Brody's expression turned serious. "Then come home. I know nothing would make our folks happier than to have you move back to Shiloh Springs. You aren't happy in Dallas, and haven't been for a long time. Don't try and kid me, it's not hard to tell you're different when you're here. You need to be around your family."

"My job's in Dallas."

"The FBI has offices in every major city. Austin isn't far away. Bet you could commute easy enough, if you wanted to." Brody leaned his hip against the car door, his arms crossed over his chest. "I can't imagine living anywhere else, especially the big city. Guess I'm a country boy at heart. I'd miss the ranch and my brothers."

Antonio stood silently at Brody's side, watching the sun begin to lower toward the horizon. Growing up, he'd loved watching the sunset from the loft in the barn; it was one of his fondest memories of living on the Boudreau ranch. He couldn't count the number of times he'd sat in the hayloft with his dad, watching the sky dissolve into a myriad of colors, neither saying a word, simply being together.

"I'll think about it."

Brody straightened. "Good. Now let's get inside. Rafe and Tessa are leaving in the morning for North Carolina, and Momma's been cooking all afternoon, putting together a send-off dinner."

"That's why I'm here. Dad called, said there'd been some trouble." Antonio studied his brother's face, trying to gauge how serious the problem with Tessa's family was, and what he could do to ease things for her and his big brother. He didn't know Tessa well, having only met her the one time he'd been home for the family barbecue, but from what his dad told him, Rafe was head over heels for the pretty schoolteacher, and Antonio would do whatever needed doing if it made his big brother happy.

"Things got a bit shaky there for a bit, but everything's fine. At least for now. There'll be a trial for Tessa's brother-in-law and her former boyfriend slash stalker, unless they take the easy way out and make a deal. Plead to lesser charges, but there's definitely going to be prison time for both. Tessa wants to tell her sister in person, says it's going to devastate her to know what he's done. She doesn't have a clue what that slimy lowlife's been doing to her sister. I think she's going to try and talk her sis into coming back to Shiloh Springs with her, at least for a while."

"Might be good for her sister to be around Tessa, and Momma will be in hog heaven having another woman around to spoil." Antonio nodded toward the house, and they started walking. The sound of voices echoed through the open front door. Rafe's laughter held a ring of happiness Antonio hadn't heard in a long time. His lips curved up at the sound, and he remembered something else, another memory from growing up at the Big House. There had been rough times, especially with each new kid that came through. But there had been so much laughter and happiness within its walls, it outweighed all the bad stuff.

A thrill of anticipation coursed through Antonio the closer each step brought him to the door. Something big waited right over the horizon, so close, but he couldn't tell what was coming. He wasn't psychic or clairvoyant, but he trusted his instincts, and they blared loud and clear—change was in the air—and his life wasn't ever going to be the same again.

Thank you for reading Rafe, Book #1 in the Texas Boudreau Brotherhood series. I hope you enjoyed Rafe and Tessa's story. Want to find out more about *Antonio Boudreau and the excitement and adventure he's about to plunge head-first into*? Keep reading for an excerpt from his book, *Antonio, Book #2 in the Texas Boudreau Brotherhood. Available at all major e-book and print vendors.*

**Antonio (Texas Boudreau Brotherhood series)
© Kathy Ivan.**

"**G**lad to have you here, Boudreau." Special Agent in Charge Derrick Williamson leaned back in his chair, his hands clasped across his stomach. Antonio studied the man, took in the freshly pressed shirt, suit pants. The top button of Williamson's shirt was undone and his tie loosened, giving off a casual vibe, but Antonio didn't buy it, not for a second.

At first glance, Williamson portrayed the easygoing, overworked FBI agent to a tee, but Antonio never went with what was obvious to the naked eye. He'd long ago learned taking things at face value often led to big mistakes, a lesson

213

he'd vowed never to repeat. Williamson appeared fit, his sandy-brown hair cut short in a businessman style. He looked like he worked out regularly, and didn't have the paunch across his middle most pencil pushers seemed to gain working in an office.

An off-white cowboy hat lay on the credenza behind Williamson, as though it had been taken off and tossed onto the surface cluttered with papers and files. Now that he could believe. Most everybody in Texas wouldn't be caught dead without their hat.

"Happy to be here. What can you tell me about the case?" He eased onto the chair opposite the desk, and propped his foot on the opposite knee, resting his own cowboy hat there. "Sounds like you've got your hands full down here."

Williamson sighed. "You've got no idea, Boudreau. Two agents out with gunshot wounds. One on maternity leave. One ruptured appendix. And two more who relocated to different cities. Leaving us in a mighty big hole we're still trying to dig our way out of. Which is why I'm glad you're here, even if it's temporary."

Looking closer, Antonio noted the dark circles under Williamson's eyes, the slightly grayish pallor to his skin. The man was obviously running on fumes, never a good idea when dealing with high profile cases or even the small stuff. A tired agent missed things.

Williamson tossed a folder across his desk. "This one's

been a pain in my backside for months. How familiar are you with James "Big Jim" Berkley?"

Antonio's brow rose at the mention of the name. Big Jim Berkley's case had been on the FBI list for years, until he'd finally been arrested, tried, and convicted two years earlier. Headline on the nightly news on every news station for months, the scandal of infighting within his family, plus the nature of his crimes provided fodder for the press, and the viewing public ate it up, spreading it across television stations until you couldn't change the channel without somebody talking about the bombings.

"I remember when he was arrested. Wasn't he caught in San Antonio? Liked to bomb synagogues, mosques, any place where minorities and people with different ideologies congregated."

Williamson leaned back in his chair, and ran a hand through his hair. "That's him alright. The man is charismatic and has a following still active to this day. Most members of his family are part of his whacked out cult. Has a bunch of rabid believers who hang on every word the idiot spouts."

Cocking his head, Antonio opened the file, and stared at the picture of James Berkley. The man was big, at least six three, maybe six four, two-hundred and fifty pounds, and it looked like it was all muscle. Salt and pepper hair. He couldn't tell from the black-and-white picture what color his eyes were, but they were cold. Empty.

"Why is the FBI looking at Berkley again? Isn't he in

federal prison serving multiple life sentences?" Antonio's eyes scanned the front page of the file, and he straightened when he noted the words "appeal granted". "This can't be right. He's getting an appeal? There was a ton of evidence against him. No way does this guy walk."

"His attorneys found some loophole, and he's trying to scurry through it like the filthy little weasel he is. At least the courts are keeping him in prison for now, until the appeal's been heard. But we've got another problem." Williamson's tone filled with disgust. "Berkley's niece was the backbone of the government's case. She provided a good chunk of the evidence used to convict Berkley. Her testimony nailed his coffin good and tight. Before the trial, she was guarded day and night. Afterwards, she went into witness protection."

Antonio quickly put two and two together, and tossed the file on the chair next to him. "Lemme guess. Berkley put a hit out on the niece to shut her up. If she can't testify, the feds case dries up, right?"

"Pretty much. Berkley's had people searching for Sharon since before the first trial. The government kept a tight lid on her throughout and whisked her away the minute she'd finished testifying, even before the verdict came down. But somehow her location was leaked and Berkley's hired goons found her in Las Vegas."

Antonio felt a clenching sensation in his gut. "She's dead?"

Williamson shook his head. "Don't know. Her next-door

neighbor ended up dead and Sharon Berkley disappeared. Vanished without a trace. Witness protection searched for months, examined every trail, every whisper of a lead, but either Berkley had her taken out—which is possible, and he's kept his mouth shut about it—or she's good enough to stay under the radar. My gut tells me Berkley's still looking for her, because I doubt he'd be able to shut up about it if he'd had her eliminated. He's too vain and thinks he's smarter than everybody involved in his case. No, we going under the assumption she's alive and hiding."

Antonio drummed his fingertips against his knee, his mind sorting through the information Williamson shared. It made sense Sharon Berkley could still be alive. But it was hard to stay completely off the grid in this day and age of electronic surveillance, computers, and facial recognition software. If she was out there, they'd find her. He only hoped it was before Big Jim Berkley did.

"What specifics can you tell me about Sharon Berkley? Last known whereabouts, any information from WITSEC? Or am I overstepping? I figure since you're telling me about Berkley's case, you want me to help locate her?"

LINKS TO PURCHASE:

www.kathyivan.com/books.html

NEWSLETTER SIGN UP

Don't want to miss out on any new books, contests, and free stuff? Sign up to get my newsletter. I promise not to spam you, and only send out notifications/e-mails whenever there's a new release or contest/giveaway. Follow the link and join today!

http://eepurl.com/baqdRX

REVIEWS ARE IMPORTANT!

People are always asking how they can help spread the word about my books. One of the best ways to do that is by word of mouth. Tell your friends about the books and recommend them. Share them on Goodreads. If you find a book or series or author you love – talk about it. Everybody loves to find out about new books and new-to-them authors, especially if somebody they know has read the book and loved it.

The next best thing is to write a review. Writing a review for a book does not have to be long or detailed. It can be as simple as saying "I loved the book."

I hope you enjoyed reading Rafe, Texas Boudreau Brotherhood.

If you liked the story, I hope you'll consider leaving a review for the book at the vendor where you purchased it and at Goodreads. Reviews are the best way to spread the word to others looking for good books. It truly helps.

BOOKS BY KATHY IVAN

www.kathyivan.com/books.html

TEXAS BOUDREAU BROTHERHOOD
Rafe

Antonio

Brody

Lucas

NEW ORLEANS CONNECTION SERIES
Desperate Choices

Connor's Gamble

Relentless Pursuit

Ultimate Betrayal

Keeping Secrets

Sex, Lies and Apple Pies

Deadly Justice

Wicked Obsession

Hidden Agenda

Spies Like Us

Fatal Intentions

New Orleans Connection Series Box Set: Books 1-3

New Orleans Connection Series Box Set: Books 4-7

CAJUN CONNECTION SERIES
Saving Sarah
Saving Savannah
Saving Stephanie
Guarding Gabi

LOVIN' LAS VEGAS SERIES
It Happened In Vegas
Crazy Vegas Love
Marriage, Vegas Style
A Virgin In Vegas
Vegas, Baby!
Yours For The Holidays
Match Made In Vegas
One Night In Vegas
Last Chance In Vegas
Lovin' Las Vegas (box set books 1-3)

OTHER BOOKS BY KATHY IVAN
Second Chances (Destiny's Desire Book #1)
Losing Cassie (Destiny's Desire Book #2)

ABOUT THE AUTHOR

USA TODAY Bestselling author Kathy Ivan spent most of her life with her nose between the pages of a book. It didn't matter if the book was a paranormal romance, romantic suspense, action and adventure thrillers, sweet & spicy, or a sexy novella. Kathy turned her obsession with reading into the next logical step, writing.

Her books transport you to the sultry splendor of the French Quarter in New Orleans in her award-winning romantic suspense, or to Las Vegas in her contemporary romantic comedies. Kathy's new romantic suspense series features, Texas Boudreau Brotherhood, features alpha heroes in small town Texas. Gotta love those cowboys!

Kathy tells stories people can't get enough of; reuniting old loves, betrayal of trust, finding kidnapped children, psychics and sometimes even a ghost or two. But one thing they all have in common – love and a happily ever after).

More about Kathy and her books can be found at

WEBSITE: www.kathyivan.com

**Follow Kathy on Facebook at
facebook.com/kathyivanauthor**

Follow Kathy on Twitter at twitter.com/@kathyivan

**Follow Kathy at BookBub
bookbub.com/profile/kathy-ivan**

Made in United States
North Haven, CT
11 May 2024

52405346R00130